God

~~Lucifer, Lucifer,~~
How You Have Fallen

By

John Kendall Seagrove

John Kendall Seagrove

KENDALL PUBLISHING
Colorado Springs, CO 80919

Lucifer, Lucifer, How You Have Fallen

Copyright © 1995 by John Kendall Seagrove

Published by Kendall Publishing
        6550 Delmonico Dr. #304
        Colorado Springs, CO 80919

Library of Congress number 95-094599

ISBN 0-9647633-0-3

Every possible effort has been made to NOT directly quote from any Bible, book, magazine or any other publication whatever. Any similarity to any published material, such as Bible verses found in any Bible translation is purely coincidental.

Printed in the United States of America

CONTENTS

PREFACE

The book you are about to read is a fictional account of the beginnings of human history. You will look at events that happened before and after time began.

You will peer into the unseen world of the spirit. You will see the beginning of evil. You will watch the creation of man.

In the pages of this book you will read of wicked spirits plotting the destruction of mankind. You will also find holy angels at work protecting us.

The books that will follow this one will portray the despair of mankind in a world dominated by sin. The salvation of man will be shown and the glorious future of the redeemed will be revealed.

Salvation of fallen man becomes the focus of all these books. God was not content to let man pay the price of his sin. He planned a way of escape for His creation.

These books are fiction. They contain many historical and Biblical facts, but they also contain fictional accounts and personal opinions of the author.

Read the Biblical scenes and regard them as the author's views of Scripture. Read the rest for what it is, fiction.

The purpose of these books is simple, to dramatically portray where we came from, what we are doing here and where we are going. They are presented with the sincere hope that they will encourage you to make the right choice as to where you will spend eternity.

We hope you enjoy reading this book and the books to follow. The next book is titled, "Man, Oh, Man, You have Fallen Too." The third book's title is "Noah, Noah, Build An Ark."

ACKNOWLEDGMENTS

I want to give thanks to my wife, Nancy, for her loving support and encouragement. She worked hard to free me from other responsibilities and give me the time needed to write these books.

She advised me and corrected me whenever it was needed. Her advice was always given with a smile. Her criticism was always given in love. Her enthusiasm and loving spirit kept me going when I felt discouraged.

Her prayers sustained me when the forces of darkness attacked me and tried to prevent these books from being written. I owe her a debt of gratitude, for whatever I accomplish that is worthwhile is, at least in part, because of her encouragement.

Several close friends and professional writers read parts of the manuscripts and offered their advice and help.

I thank God for sending His holy angels to protect me and my wife while these books were being written.

I especially thank the Holy Spirit for inspiring me. He planted the thoughts and ideas in my mind and heart that are found on these pages.

Although much of the material in these books is fiction, I firmly believe the Holy Spirit guided my thoughts in writing them. I think a fair picture is presented of what goes on in the spirit world to influence what happens in the physical world.

Please understand, no attempt is made to claim the kind of inspiration found in the writings of the prophets and apostles who gave us the Bible. Only that inspiration given to authors, artists, musicians and other who produce works they could not have done otherwise is claimed.

To God be the glory and to you, dear reader, be the blessings and encouragements found in these pages.

INTRODUCTION

Beyond the veil of this flesh there is a world unseen by human eyes, a world seen only when the eyes of one's spirit are opened.

It is a world more real than this physical world. It existed before this planet was formed, before ever a man walked on the earth. It will continue to exist long after the last man has left his footprints in the sands of time.

Few have ventured to look beyond the veil and see things hidden from most of mankind. Fewer still have crossed over into that realm and returned to tell us what they have seen.

You are invited to draw aside that veil and gaze into the eternal realm. Come with me on a journey through time and space. We go back in time, back beyond the middle ages, beyond the pyramids, beyond the Great Flood, beyond Eden, back to a time in eternity past.

There we will meet the archenemy of mankind, the one who plotted the downfall of the human race. We will see his self-deception and his deception of angels.

Through the endless reaches of space we will travel to a tiny planet, satellite of a small star, in a minor galaxy, floating somewhere in one of the billions of universes whirling in a super-universe that is itself a speck of light and matter in a super-super-universe.

On this planet we call "earth," God created a man and a woman. He gave them dominion over the earth and told them to be fruitful and multiply. We will glimpse scenes from the history of man on this planet. We will look beyond the sights and sounds of the physical world and watch Satan and his evil forces working their witchcraft to destroy the earth and its inhabitants.

But for now, let's go back and view some of the things that led to the beginning as we know it.

Chapter One

Lucifer Wants More

Lucifer walked slowly back and forth, turning this way and that, viewing himself in the giant mirror that had just been installed in his palatial home. It was huge, measuring two hundred feet wide and fifty feet high. It made the room seem even larger, adding a dimension that gave one a spectacular feeling of grandeur.

The splendor of it all was exceeded only by the dazzling beauty of the one admiring himself, gazing proudly upon his image so wonderfully mirrored there. It was almost an act of worship as he adored the reflection of himself.

"Ah, Lucifer, you are indeed the most beautiful person in all creation." He spoke the words clearly and with great feeling so his ears could savor the sound of them. A thought rose up in his mind, "Wouldn't it be wonderful to hear others say those words to me?

"Yes," he said, "I deserve to be praised. I even deserve to be worshiped. After all, has not the Almighty Himself called me 'Light Bearer' and 'Covering Cherub' and 'Guardian Angel'?"

Turning to face directly into the mirror, Lucifer gazed intently at the image of himself. "I am absolutely perfect," he exclaimed, "and I am clothed with diamonds, rubies, emeralds and sapphires, but even the most beautiful jewels cannot compare with my beauty.

"I blaze with light. I am filled with wisdom. I am at home in the garden of God. I approach the mountain of God. I even walk among the stones of fire. I am called

'Son of the Morning.'

"I deserve to be worshiped. I deserve to rule. That's it! I deserved to rule. I will rule the angels. I will occupy the highest throne. I will preside over the Assembly. I will exalt myself to be as great as Him. Maybe I will even be greater than Him."

For a moment he stood still, admiring himself and thinking there must be a way to design more splendid and impressive clothing for one so important. Then he paced about, discontent with the way things were.

That new mirror helped him see things more clearly. Yes, it was becoming more and more clear. He had wanted more power, more authority for a long time. He should be able to make laws and force others to obey them. The right to control the work, the activities and affections of others should be his.

Lucifer left the mirrored banquet room and walked down a long hallway, through the massive kitchen and out the back door. Across the expensively decorated stones of the servants' patio and past the gorgeous flowers bordering it he strode. These things meant nothing to him.

Moving through a jewel-encrusted gate, he entered a garden of incredible size and beauty. It was a mile wide and a mile and a half long. Pathways of pure marble intertwined throughout the entire garden. Exquisite pieces of ivory decorated the edges of the paths. Jewels of every description were polished and set in gold so pure it was almost transparent.

Massive beds of flowers exuded a variety of fragrances as he walked the marbled pathways. Multi-tiered levels of flowers added more beauty to forests of trees and bushes growing up out of the most perfect grass that never needs mowing.

Lucifer reached the end of the garden and passed through a gate made of ivory that was decorated with rubies and pearls. Across a large meadow he walked and up to a promontory overlooking the beautiful sea that bordered his enormous property. It was a large rock that rose above the waters like a sentinel. It was pure gold. He sat down on it and looked at the distant horizon. His thoughts became melancholy.

He surveyed the shoreline to the right and to the left and then spoke out loud. "This is the end of my property," he said. "I should own that water also. I am worthy to possess more, much more. There is no limit to what I should have."

Rising from the golden rock, he stepped down and walked a few paces. Turning about and looking back, he slowly shook his head from side to side. An expression of disdain spread over his face.

"A rock," he muttered, "I sit on a rock while He sits on a throne. I deserve a throne. I deserve to be worshiped. I deserve to rule over the angels. They should kneel at my feet and make their requests."

On the long walk back to his house, his eyes looked downward. His countenance was fallen. His face was sullen and his thoughts gloomy. A feeling of dejection crept over him.

Lucifer's feet didn't feel the soft, yet firm response of the grass as he plodded on through the meadow. His nose did not smell the fragrance of the flowers that grew in wild profusion there. His ears did not hear the gentle sounds of heavenly music that filled the air.

Resentment and bitterness caused him to think only of greater things that he deserved and of the perfection with which he had so long and faithfully performed his duties for the Throne. He had expertly organized all of the choirs.

He had wisely chosen exactly the right choirs for each occasion.

Lucifer conversed with himself as he walked along. "I brought sweet music up from inside my soul. I composed it and inscribed it with great care. I fashioned majestic words of praise and worship and joined them to the music. I instructed the many choir directors to bring forth the finest performances of my music.

"When the choirs gathered together for a special celebration, I conducted them myself. I led them to perfection in praising and worshiping before His throne.

"Why should He be the only one to receive worship? Why should total allegiance be given to Him? Am I not worthy to receive a little praise? Have I not done great things? Am I not perfect in beauty and wisdom? I plan the perfect praise and worship programs. I schedule every brilliant performance He enjoys so much.

"Those low-class angels jump and shout with excitement when their turn comes to sing and fall down at His feet. Couldn't they give a little of their adoration to me? I am, after all, their chief leader.

"The ingratitude of those choir directors is unforgivable. I asked one to bring some of his singers and musicians to one of my banquets. All I asked was that they give a little praise and worship to me and what did he say? 'Sir, that would be inappropriate.'

"Well, I guess I showed him. I demoted him to the position of twenty-ninth harpist and made the angel he replaced director. You should have heard their next performance before the Throne without any words and music from me. They did their best, but it was pitiful, sincere but pitiful. I guess you would call it 'a joyful noise unto the Lord.' Ha, Ha, Ha, Haaaa! I wonder what He thought?"

Approaching the outer gate of the garden, his steps quickened. His face looked more determined. His eyes blazed with anger. He could not wait to get back to the house. Rising above the trees, he flew swiftly the last mile and a half.

Entering the house, he shouted, "Rowan! Rowan! Where are you? Come here!" Lucifer's voice rang sharply down the great hallway.

The Chief Butler came out of his office and responded, "Yes sir, what is it?"

"I want you to summon all the commanders of the Third Estate to a banquet. I want them to be impressed." He cautioned, "Do not invite any captains or generals. They ask too many questions."

Rowan inquired, "What occasion shall I tell them it is for? They will surely ask a reason."

Lucifer replied, "Tell them I have a wonderful surprise for them. Now, schedule this banquet as soon as you can. I want to do this as quickly as possible. Urge them to come at the earliest time available."

"Yes sir, I'll start making the arrangements right away," answered Rowan as he turned to walk back toward his office. "I'll let you know the time when I return."

Lucifer walked up the hallway and into the banquet room to look again at the newly installed mirror. He stepped up close and smiled at the image he saw there. He watched the image smile and move in response to him. "I wish the other angels would obey me as instantly and completely as you do," he said.

Turning from the mirror, Lucifer walked quickly to his magnificent office where he planned his work and wrote the music for the many choirs and orchestras.

It was a large office, measuring forty by eighty feet. A number of high ranking angels could gather and be seated comfortably in the plush chairs arranged so that each one faced the executive chair at the desk.

The desk was huge, twelve feet wide and six feet deep. The top of the desk was three feet from the floor. Lucifer had been created perfect and was exactly seven feet tall, so he was very comfortable at a desk of such proportions.

He sat down in the large executive chair and began immediately to organize the unholy thoughts that had been swimming around in his mind for some time now. An outline of the proposal he would present to the commanders was soon written on the paper before him.

It was a masterful plan, one that would surely win the enthusiastic support of all the commanders. Once he had their allegiance, he could then persuade the captains and generals to support his plan. Yes, Lucifer could just imagine it now, the entire Third Estate under his feet, acknowledging him as god.

He would rule with an iron hand. He would whip them into a fighting force that could conquer the other estates and he would crown himself Lord of all.

This brief outline would not reveal all of his plans, though, just enough to enlist the desire for advancement and power in the commanders. It would promise them great things, while concealing his scheme to enslave them and force them to do his bidding.

It was just a piece of paper with a few words written on it, but oh, what words. They would change the course of events in all of creation forever.

Once something is created, it can never be completely destroyed. It can be forgiven and treated by the merciful judgment of God as if it had never happened, but the fact that it happened remains.

That paper would be collected as evidence and stored in the eternal vaults of heaven as a witness to all created beings of how pride can rise in the hearts of men and angels. If pride is not confessed and submitted to the mercy of God, it can grow until it turns the soul against God.

When that happens, pride can agitate and prod the mind until it forces one to make a decision to submit to God and ask for His mercy and advice or to exalt self against God and follow one's own will.

Lucifer was walking on the pathway of pride, farther and farther toward the point of no return. He would soon fall over the precipice of eternal rebellion.

As the outline of apostasy took shape on the paper, Lucifer congratulated himself on his ability to organize such a bold plan. He reveled in the knowledge that this was entirely his own idea. He had originated it. He had developed it. Now, he himself was preparing to present it to many of the leading angels of heaven.

At last he had found a way to not only direct the activities of vast multitudes of angels, he could now, if successful, begin to demand that they worship him. "Ah yes," he muttered, "soon I will receive the worship I deserve.

"They will not only obey me as their archangel, they will worship me as their god. I will be equal to Him. I will rule them as a god, not as His servant. Maybe, just maybe, if I can get enough power, I will depose Him and rule over all creation. If not, at least I will capture several of His universes and rule them, apart from Him."

Lucifer read the few short lines on the paper again, changing a word or two to create just the right effect. He knew that if the commanders rejected his proposal it would be impossible to carry out his plan to establish a separate kingdom.

When he was satisfied, he left the paper on the desk, rose and walked proudly back into the banquet hall. Approaching the mirror, he held his head high, his mouth forming a half smile. He looked into the mirror for a moment and then spoke. "Lucifer, you are a genius," he said. "You are destined for great things."

He strode confidently across the room to the platform where the head table would be placed for the banquet. He practiced a few gestures and a few words that he would use to persuade the commanders to follow him in his rebellion.

As he stood there, rehearsing his thoughts, he could almost see the commanders sitting at the tables listening to him and growing ever more eager to grasp the opportunity for promotion and power.

"Yes," he whispered to himself, "it will be a great banquet and a grand beginning of my own kingdom. My throne will be more glorious than His. My rule will be absolute. No longer will I bow before Him. Everyone will bow at my feet and worship me."

****

Rowan was busy contacting all the commanders of the Third Estate, that group of angels of which Lucifer was the leader, the archangel. He diligently performed his assignment, but somehow, he had an uneasy feeling about it. Why didn't Lucifer tell him the purpose of the banquet? He was having a difficult time convincing some of them to come to a special banquet if they could not know its purpose.

Arriving at the home of Elmordal, he was ushered into an office decorated to befit the power of this high official. Everything about that office seemed powerful and strong. The angel sitting behind the massive desk looked very impressive. He was Commander over seven million angels.

"Greetings, Rowan, what brings you here?" he inquired, motioning for his visitor to sit in the heavy upholstered chair in front of the desk.

"Lucifer is giving a very special banquet," said Rowan, "and is inviting all the commanders of the Third Estate to attend. It will be fabulous. He greatly desires your presence there."

"What is the purpose of this big banquet?" asked Elmordal. "What could be so important that he would invite all of the commanders to attend?"

"I don't know," replied Rowan. "He said it would be a great surprise. I fact, he wouldn't even tell me and I am to plan the whole thing. I wonder how I can select the food. How can I even plan appropriate decorations if I don't know the purpose of the banquet?"

"Well, I don't want to seem offensive to a superior angel," said Elmordal, "but I have too much vital work to do right now. Not only that, I just can't see going to a big meeting if he can't even tell me why.

"Do you remember that time he asked one of the choir directors to bring his people and worship him? I was greatly offended when I heard about that. I have no intention of being part of that kind of thing.

"Rowan, I can't tell you what to do, but please let me give you some friendly advice. Take care how you obey Lucifer. He may punish you for disobeying him, but that is better than disobeying God."

Elmordal continued, "Remember, God is the Creator.

He created all of us. He has the right and the authority to make the rules. We may not understand some of His rules, but we must never, never willfully disobey Him.

"If Lucifer commands you to do something that you know is in disobedience to God, I suggest you disobey Lucifer. That choir director refused Lucifer's request and was demoted and humiliated, but I am sure God knows about it and will someday see that justice is done.

"Please give my regrets to Lucifer and tell him that I am in the final stages of the Bindowr project and my captain will be filing an update very soon."

"Thank you, Elmordal," said Rowan. "Several other top-ranking commanders have said things similar to what you have just told me. I am Lucifer's chief butler and I am in a very responsible and delicate position, but I will accept your advice and carefully evaluate his orders from now on.

"You have helped me realize that my first allegiance is to our Creator and that all other obedience must be performed only if it pleases Him. We all make mistakes from time to time, but that is different from deliberate disobedience."

He concluded by saying, "That can lead to rebellion and I shudder to think of what the consequences of that might be. It would at least break the sweet fellowship of His Spirit that fills us with His love and life. I don't even want to think about it."

Rowan stood up and prepared to leave. Thanking Elmordal again for his advice, he turned and followed the butler to the front door. Bidding the butler farewell, he departed and continued on his way to invite the few remaining commanders to the banquet that was looming in his mind as a curious mystery.

He completed his assignment and returned to report that

an agreeable time had been found and that most of the commanders would be present and eager to discover the great surprise. "I'm sorry to report that not all of the commanders will be able to attend," he said. "Some of them are extremely busy with work they just cannot leave right now. Perhaps if…"

"What do you mean, they cannot attend?" roared Lucifer. "Didn't you impress them with the importance of this banquet? I sent you out to do a job. You have failed! You go into your office and write down the names of every one of them that refused my invitation. I will deal with them and you later. Right now I want you to get busy and make this the biggest and best banquet you have ever planned."

"Sir, about the decorations and the…"

"Get out! Get out!" shouted Lucifer. "Must I do everything myself? Your days as Chief Butler are numbered. Get out of my sight. Don't you speak to me again until you have this banquet ready. I have more important things to think about than decorations."

Rowan retreated to his office, convinced that Elmordal's advice would be needed soon. Lucifer was not only causing him serious concern, but other angels were beginning to notice that things were not going well in this house.

But, for now, he occupied himself with the problem of what food to plan and what decorations to select. If only he could know the purpose of the banquet, he could make sure everything would be just right.

"Let's see," he mused, "food disguised so that one must taste it to know what it is. Then, a blaze of various colors in the decorations and a euphony of indistinct music to add to the mystery of the occasion. That would keep the guests from guessing the purpose of the banquet until Lucifer chose to announce it. Surely that would please him, wouldn't it?"

Rowan's thoughts turned to the threats Lucifer had made. "I think maybe it is time for me to have a talk with Bermijon," he whispered to himself. "I want to find out how I might be assigned to another job. It won't be easy. We may have to appeal to the Throne. Well, whatever, I'm not going to stay here and let this situation get any worse.

"Elmordal was right," Rowan remembered. "My first allegiance is to God. If I must choose between obedience to Lucifer and the rules God has established, I must always choose to obey God.

"He is the Creator and I must do whatever it takes to please Him. The wonderful joy, the sweet aroma, the beautiful music, the life-giving presence of His Spirit in me are more important than anything Lucifer can give me.

"And what has Lucifer given me? Threats! I'm going to see Bermijon as soon as possible."

Chapter Two

A Plot Revealed

It was a spectacular banquet. Rowan had poured his best efforts into it. As he watched the commanders gathering in the large banquet hall, he noted their reactions to the decor.

He listened with warm satisfaction as he overheard some of their comments. They were completely unable to guess the purpose of the event by viewing the decorations or the food.

The placement of the tables offered no clue either. The commanders were having a delightful time discussing what might be the secret reason for this extravagant affair.

Romer, Midgaren and Hartmorel were standing near Rowan and he could hear them speaking. "I wonder if Lucifer will make his announcement before we eat or after?" said Midgaren.

"I predict it will be after," suggested Hartmorel. He saw Rowan standing nearby and inquired, "Can't you give us just a hint of what this is all about?"

"Sorry," shrugged Rowan, "Lucifer hasn't even told me yet. I do hope his announcement will be something good. Have you noticed that even the music offers no help in guessing what it will be? That is because I don't know what it will be."

Most of the guests had now arrived. The room was nearly full. Pleasant chatter filled the air and mingled with the music. The food was ready. Rowan walked to the front of the room and signaled for silence. Genribben was asked to lead in thanks.

"Eternal God," he said, bowing his head, "You have created all things. You have created the food we are about to eat. We know not the occasion for this food, but we give You thanks for it and for those who have prepared it. We thank You for Rowan, who has so cleverly disguised it that we cannot identify it until we taste it. May Your life-giving power permeate this food as we partake. May we be blessed by it and may our hearts be ever grateful to You for the many ways You continually bless us. Amen."

The commanders sat at tables prepared for twelve. The food was in large dishes on each table so that the entire group of one thousand six hundred seventy-nine angels could be served quickly. Two servers were stationed at each table to attend to the needs and requests of the guests.

Just then, Lucifer entered and without a word went straight to the head table and sat at the center place. He had been just outside the main door when thanks to God for the food was being given.

He had muttered to himself, "They should be thanking me for the food. It all came from my gardens, yet they bow their heads like wimps and thank Him for it. When I am god they will have to thank me for every scrap of food they put into their mouths."

Right now, Lucifer didn't feel hungry, so he refused the food that was offered him. He watched the six commanders sitting at his table, eating and chatting among themselves. He had hand picked them. They would be promoted to the rank of general. They would help him convince the captains and generals to follow him.

Lucifer's thoughts were interrupted by Sinberol, who was seated immediately to his left. "What is the big surprise you have for us," he queried.

"You will find out soon enough," Lucifer replied. Somehow, Lucifer's warped mind regarded that innocent question as a challenge to his intent to have absolute control of others.

"You must learn to trust me," he continued. "I have great plans for you, but I must know that you will trust me in everything. You must not question me. You must believe that I know what is best. I will give you great rewards but you must do what I say without question. You must always submit to my authority. Otherwise, I cannot use you."

Sinberol turned and continued eating, but his thoughts were somewhat troubled. Lucifer was such a powerful angel, with such great authority, that a mere commander might not understand his determination to pursue the successful achievement of his goals. Still, there was something in the tone of Lucifer's voice that didn't sound just right. It sounded dictatorial and paranoid. Sinberol wondered what to do.

The meal was a huge success. The food was devoured with great relish. Adjoining tables competed to see who could identify all of the many disguised foods first. Winners rose and were cheered with loud applause and shouts of approval.

Friends inquired about the progress of various projects and offered advice and encouragement. Promises to visit more often were made. Recent promotions and advancements were warmly cheered.

Servers began clearing the tables as the slower angels finished the last morsels on their plates. When all was in order, Rowan walked to the front and announced that Lucifer would speak. Applause swept across the vast room as Lucifer rose to his feet.

He looked over the crowd for a moment as paranoid thoughts raced through his mind. Not only had thirty-six commanders refused his invitation, thirteen of those who promised to come had not shown up. He counted the thirteen empty seats. He would have Rowan get their names. Why hadn't they come?

All eyes were focused on Lucifer. The commanders were eagerly waiting to hear what he had to say.

"You all seem to be enjoying yourselves," he said. "I have called you here to show you how you can increase your success. I have plans that include every one of you and all of the angels under your command.

"Perhaps you have noticed that the best assignments have been going to the other estates. Have you ever wondered why? I have. I have been speaking up for you and requesting better assignments to come our way. I am not happy with the answers I have been getting.

"There are whole universes out there to be explored and conquered. Each one of you commands several million angels. Think of the countless numbers of creatures in just one universe. You should be ruling them.

"You were created to be like Him. Shouldn't you act like Him? Why should you be content to wait until orders come down through the chain of command to you? You should be promoted to much higher positions and given much greater authority.

"He wants to keep you down here at this level forever. He doesn't want you to attain your full potential. Mandabar, how long have you been Commander of the eighty-ninth district? Don't you think that it is about time you were given the honor and recognition you deserve? I have great plans for you, Mandabar.

"And you, Esparel, when was the last time you had a

promotion? Come with me, Esparel, and I will make you great."

The fact that Lucifer himself granted or approved all promotions in the Third Estate was ignored.

Lucifer continued, "You six commanders here at the table with me, you will occupy high offices in the kingdom I am planning. I will give you honors greater than you have ever dreamed of, honors that you will never receive as long as we keep on slaving for Him.

"I have a plan and I want to share it with you now. I have written a few things down. Listen carefully. The things you are about to hear will change your lives forever. This piece of paper will be known as the document that changed the fortunes of the Third Estate. I know you will agree that the time for action has come. I think you will agree that here are the things we must do:

"ONE---we must commit ourselves to establishing our own kingdom. We will build it. We will rule it. We will make our own rules instead of simply obeying every order that comes down from above. We will achieve greater power and glory than we will ever get here.

"TWO---we must organize ourselves into a fighting force that can win. We must obtain the absolute loyalty of every angel under our command. We will encounter opposition, but we must be prepared to overcome it.

"THREE---we must gain the willing cooperation of key officers in the other estates. If they oppose us, we will defeat them.

"FOUR---when we have enough power, I will demand a separate kingdom for us. He cannot refuse us. He made us to rule. It is our destiny. We must arise and fulfill our destiny.

"You see? It is so simple. We can do it. You can do it.

27

I want you to be the best you can be. I want you to assume your rightful places of honor and glory. Will you do it? Are you with me?"

Shouts, cheers and thunderous applause erupted all over the great banquet hall. A standing ovation of enthusiastic approval swelled for several minutes.

Lucifer's eyes scanned the audience and noticed that some commanders were not standing or applauding. Sinberol, right there next to Lucifer, remained seated.

As the applause subsided and the commanders sat down, Sinberol rose to his feet and said, "Sir, I have a very uncomfortable feeling about all this. If any of us are unhappy in our present positions, we should organize our requests and submit them through the proper channels."

Lucifer glared at Sinberol and was about to give him a severe tongue-lashing but he restrained himself. These commanders could not be forced to join with him. Neither could they be forced to obey him---not yet.

The room suddenly became silent. Every ear was listening to hear what Lucifer would say. With a cunning that was deceptive even to those close by, Lucifer erased the glare from his eyes and spoke with a compassion in his voice that seemed to portray genuine concern and care for Sinberol's future.

"Sinberol," he spoke in gentle tones, yet loud enough to be heard by everyone in the room, "if you do not go with us, what do you think will become of you? How will the angels you direct and care for react? Do you think they will respect a quitter? Do you think they will continue to obey you? They will surely leave you and come with us.

"And then what will you do? Where will you go? Do you really think you can join one of the other estates? Do you honestly believe they will welcome a traitor into their midst?

"Sinberol, you must decide. You must decide NOW! Do you want to come with us and receive great riches, honor, power and authority? Or, can you stand there and truthfully say that you want to throw away your entire future and become a despised outcast forever?"

All eyes shifted their gaze from Lucifer to Sinberol. All ears strained to hear if there would be a response. A moment of intense silence charged the air with anticipation.

Sinberol had been studying the face and eyes of Lucifer. He had been listening ever so carefully to the words being spoken, trying to evaluate whether things would really happen as Lucifer was saying they would. An eternal decision was made.

Commander Sinberol turned his gaze away from Lucifer, turned his head to the left, then shifted his body to the left, turning his back to Lucifer. He looked toward the end of the great hall and lifted his right hand out in front of him. With his forefinger he began counting the few empty seats at some of the far tables. He spoke not a word.

Spinzarel, one of the wisest and most honored of the commanders, was seated at a table near the middle of the banquet room. He rose and spoke slowly, choosing his words carefully. "Lucifer, I consider you my dear friend. You have asked my advice on several matters in the past. Please hear me now. This plan to set up a kingdom of your own, apart from the Almighty God, is not a good idea, It will…"

A chorus of boos and shouts of "Sit down!" rose from the crowd and drowned out his words. He remained standing, but did not try to speak any more.

Sinberol looked in that direction. After a moment, he walked over to Spinzarel. The two of them turned and began walking toward the main door.

A buzz of whispered conversations swept across the room as they walked out. Lucifer stood silent and glared at them.

Rowan, who had been standing near the entrance and felt the brush of their clothing as they passed by, suddenly stepped into an open space between two tables and shouted with a voice that rang loud and clear throughout the great hall. "Lucifer, I shall not serve as your butler any longer. I am going with them." He turned and walked quickly out shouting, "Spinzarel, Sinberol, wait for me!"

As the commanders turned their attention back to Lucifer, another one stood up, then another and another. With determined faces and sad hearts they made their way to the door. Several more rose and followed, away from Lucifer's palace, back to their homes.

Lucifer spoke in a cool, deliberate voice. "Does anyone else want to leave? This matter is not for cowards. If you want to lose what you have and all you ever hope to have, get up and leave now. I want angels with courage. I want commanders who can lead their troops to victory. I promise you that I will give you rewards beyond your wildest dreams. I promise you that we will establish a kingdom like no other."

Sixteen hundred fifty-eight commanders remained seated. After a moment of silence, Saddramman stood up and shouted, "Lucifer, we pledge our loyalty to you. We pledge the angels we command to your service. We will follow you wherever you go. We renounce our allegiance to Him. We give our allegiance to you. Lead on Lucifer, Bearer of Light, lead us on."

A roar of approval erupted. The crowd jumped to its feet. Commanders of every rank rushed forward and bowed down before Lucifer. Enthusiastic praises flowed for some time. It was evident that many angels in the Third Estate had been dissatisfied for a long while.

When the wild demonstration calmed and the commanders returned to their tables, Lucifer gave them their first instructions, brief and to the point. "I want you to get your angels together and train them to be the strongest, most powerful soldiers in all creation. Demand their absolute loyalty. If any of them show signs of weakness, throw them out. We have a great task ahead of us. We can do it. We will do it. We must not fail."

With that, Lucifer dismissed the commanders and stepped down to mingle with them. Most of them departed after offering brief courtesies on their way toward the main door. The five commanders who had shared the head table with Lucifer remained for some time, inquiring what they should be doing.

Lucifer informed them that they should each make a list of more than three hundred commanders. They should contact each one on their lists and make sure each one was doing his job well. However, their first task would be to contact the seventy uncommitted commanders and convince them to join the others in this most important project.

"Impress them emphatically," said Lucifer, "that failing to join means passing up the greatest opportunity they will ever have. To fail to join with us means giving up their entire future. Their present positions will be dissolved. Their angels will forsake them to join us. Tell those commanders who will not join us that they will be considered traitors. They will be lonely, forsaken outcasts forever."

Lucifer paused for a moment, wondering if he should

say any more. Yes, these five commanders needed to hear more. They must be able to frighten the other commanders and all of their angels into joining.

All those words spoken earlier about throwing out the cowards were only designed to impress the commanders and inspire an enthusiastic dedication to himself. Lucifer's real goal at this point was to draw as many angels as possible away from God by any and every means.

Lucifer's eyes blazed. His face darkened. His mouth curled into a snarl. He said, "You tell every one of those who humiliated me by walking out, as well as those who did not attend, that when we take over there will be reprisals.

"There is no way they can hide from us. I will personally proscribe them. I will order punishments upon them that are too horrible to even think about. Their only hope for their eternal future is to come to their senses and join us."

He straightened to his full height of seven feet and lowered his voice to almost a whisper, a whisper dripping with venom. The look in his eyes and the sound of his voice sent chilling waves of fear through all five of them. There was something in the words they were about to hear that threatened terrible punishments to each of them if they failed.

Looking down at them, his eyes burning into the very soul of each one, he spoke. "I want every angel in the entire Third Estate to join us. It is up to you five commanders to make it happen. I am holding you responsible to see that it does happen. Listen carefully to me. I do not like failure. I will not tolerate failure. Do not fail."

Lucifer turned and walked away to his office, leaving

the five commanders stunned and bewildered, wondering what they had gotten themselves into.

They left the palace, noting that the butler was not there to bid them farewell. In silence they walked down the broad path that led to the main road. Out onto the road they proceeded and continued silently for a while, each one occupied with his own thoughts about what had just happened.

It was Berlion who spoke first. "I believe we should seek some advice about what we are doing. Let's be sure we are not making a big mistake."

Gudreber said, "Yes, I agree. It sounded to me like we were being asked to make an eternal decision. Can you imagine the consequences if we make a wrong decision?"

Milnahten replied, "Can you just imagine the consequences of leaving Lucifer if he is successful? You saw the look in his eyes. You heard the implied threats in his voice. He is the most powerful angel in the Third Estate. He is the archangel. Can you seriously consider opposing him?"

Ginzbarel added, "I wouldn't want to be in your shoes when Lucifer takes over. And, I believe he will take over. I have never known him to fail in anything he has ever done."

A brief moment of silence followed. Yenthapen had been weighing everything that was being said. He then asked, "Has Lucifer ever led us into anything wrong? He is without question the greatest and most influential angel in all of the Third Estate.

"He is our ruler, our great Commander. We work for him. All that we have, all of our authority, all of the angels under our command, our homes, our possessions, everything, comes from him."

Yenthapen continued, "To desert him and try to join one of the other estates would be nothing less than treason. We are under his command. We must do as he orders us to do. If he is wrong, then he will answer to the Almighty. We cannot be blamed for simply following orders."

Stopping and directly confronting the two, he said, "Berlion, Gudreber, my advice to you is to forget your treasonous thoughts and return to loyalty, obedience and dedicated service. Nobody respects a quitter. Nobody trusts a traitor. I suggest that you get busy and do what Lucifer ordered us to do. Remember, he will not tolerate failure.

"I will personally watch both of you and I will report your progress or lack thereof to Lucifer."

Another moment of silence. Berlion's mind digested what Yenthapen had said and tried to decide which way to go, with Lucifer and the prospect of power and riches, or to rebel against him and risk losing everything.

While he thought on these things, Berlion noted that the joy of the presence of God's Spirit was gone. He could no longer hear the sweet music emanating from himself, the trees, the flowers.

He could no longer smell the fragrant aroma that permeates all that has the life of God in it. He wondered about those things for a moment and then made an eternal decision.

"I shall seek advice from the highest counsel I can find," Berlion announced. "I shall request audience with the Almighty Himself if I have to. I will not make a decision like this without obtaining the best advice available to me. My eternal future is at stake.

"I must never forget that Almighty God created me. Lucifer is not my God. He did not create me. I must never bow down and worship anyone but Him who created me."

Berlion continued, "If Lucifer's plan to establish a separate kingdom is approved by the Almighty, then I shall cooperate to the best of my ability and urge my angels to do so as well. But, if it is not, I want nothing to do with it.

"If Lucifer considers me a traitor, then I shall trust my Creator to protect me from him. I really don't think Lucifer can oppose the One who created him. I think his plan is wrong. I don't think he can possibly succeed. I am going to try to get an appointment to see Michael, archangel of the First Estate."

"Me too," said Gudreber. "I am going with you, Berlion. We will go together. Something like this is too important to just enter into without seeking good advice."

Berlion and Gudreber bade farewell to the others and turned into the street where Hazbeger lived. They would waste no time. They would ask him to use his influence to get an appointment for them with the highest official he could reach.

Chapter Three

Defection

Hazbeger was a very important and knowledgeable angel in the Third Estate. He had high-level contacts in both the First and Second Estates.

Berlion and Gudreber entered the front gate and walked up the long curved path to Hazbeger's house. It was a large house, set toward the front of massive gardens filled with trees arranged in winding rows. Exquisite flower beds were banked on both sides of wide pebbled pathways.

Crystal pools dotted the landscape behind the house and were inhabited by water creatures of every description. About one-half mile from the house was the rear gate. It was entirely made of pearl and decorated with red and blue gemstones.

Vegetables and a great variety of spices and herbs were growing in separate gardens. Fruit trees were scattered throughout the whole property, while bushes laden with berries grew in clusters here and there.

A small hill rose toward the rear of the property, giving a view of several other mansions spread over a broad sweeping valley. Hazbeger often climbed to the top of that hill to view the valley and the majestic mountains beyond.

Berlion and Gudreber approached the front door of the house and were greeted by Merilon the butler. He ushered them into the drawing room and went to notify Hazbeger.

Neither of them had ever visited there, so they looked about and commented on the decor. The room was furnished in simple, yet expensive taste. The chairs were not massive but were sturdy in construction. A large couch sat on one side of the room, beckoning one to lie down and rest upon its firm but comfortable cushion. Pictures on the walls blended into the mood of the room.

Hazbeger strode in, smiling and greeting Berlion and Gudreber as if he had been expecting them. He sat down, facing them, and waited for them to speak.

Berlion said, "Hazbeger, we need your help. Will you help us get an appointment to see Michael the archangel?"

"You don't need to see Michael," he replied. "I know why you are here and I can advise you, but please let me hear what you have to say."

Gudreber leaned forward and spoke rapidly. "Lucifer is calling all angels of the Third Estate to follow him in establishing a separate kingdom in which he will be equal to the Almighty One. We think it is a bad idea and we want to transfer to one of the other estates. Can you help us?"

"I can arrange to have you transferred," replied Hazbeger. "I have been watching Lucifer's activities for some time and I can see that if he keeps pursuing that plan it will end in tragedy.

"As a matter of fact, I have already started the process whereby all of the angels of the Third Estate who wish to do so may transfer away from Lucifer without fear of reprisal.

"Lucifer's desire to be equal with the Almighty God simply cannot be accomplished. Lucifer cannot create anything. He himself is a created being.

"There can be only one God. Lucifer can never be almighty. He can never be equal to God. There is and always will be only one God. It cannot be otherwise."

"That brings up an interesting question," said Berlion. "I heard about an angel named Peglar who was permitted to stand before the Throne and speak directly to God. He is reported to have said that he tried to look into the dazzling light that radiated from the Throne and thought he saw three persons there. If that is true, then are there not already three Gods?"

"No!" said Hazbeger. "There is one God. How He reveals Himself is beyond our comprehension. I do not know how He can be three and yet one. He has been called 'The Father,' The Word' and The Spirit,' yet He is One.

"I suggest you attend a lecture by Ergard Luminal, one of the great teachers in the First Estate. He gives the best explanation of the nature and expression of the Godhead that I have ever heard.

"However, that question can wait. Right now we must get you away from Lucifer. I suggest that the two of you contact as many of the commanders as you can who do not support Lucifer's plan and encourage them to see me as soon as possible.

"When we see how many commanders and angels want to transfer, we will present our request through the proper channels and make this transition as smooth as possible. I and several other commanders already have the preliminary paperwork submitted to the authorities.

"I will certainly be sad to lose my house and my beautiful gardens, but I am sure the Creator will provide for all of us. One of the commanders made an interesting comment while I was talking with him about this transfer. He said, 'Eyes have not seen, nor ears heard, what God has prepared for them that love Him.' I take that to mean the Creator will bless us for choosing to be faithful to Him in the face of great temptation."

Hazbeger concluded by saying, "I will add your names to the list of those requesting transfer. With all of those who may not want to follow their commanders in Lucifer's plot, we will have many millions of angels to help find their places in the other estates."

Berlion grasped Hazbeger's hand and said, "Thank you so much for helping us. We didn't know where to turn, but we felt confident that you could advise us. We will do our best to help you save as many millions of angels from Lucifer's rebellion as possible."

Gudreber added, "I'm really frightened at the thought of what might happen because of all this."

"Just be sure of this," assured Hazbeger, "if you keep your loyalties pointed toward the One who occupies the Throne, you will always be cared for by His love and tender mercy. He created you. He loves you and you can depend on Him to do what is best for you."

Berlion and Gudreber bade farewell to Hazbeger and departed, rejoicing and feeling much better about their future. They were determined to see as many commanders as they could about the transfer.

Meanwhile, the great majority of the commanders in the Third Estate were busy planning how they might obey Lucifer's orders to regiment their troops into an invincible force.

Gutzebom, Commander of the twentieth district, called a mass meeting of the millions of angels that reported to him to outline Lucifer's plan to them. His lieutenants arranged them by order and waited for him to speak.

His speech was short and to the point. He outlined the plan for a separate kingdom in clear terms.

Two lieutenants stood and objected. They said they wanted no part of such a scheme. After severe threats and much ridicule from the other angels, they walked out. Most of their angels followed them. Some did not.

Gathering soldiers who would pledge their loyalty to Lucifer did not take long. Some of the commanders who had not attended the banquet were persuaded to join, while others could not be moved from their resolve to abandon Lucifer. The twelve original generals and all one hundred and forty-four captains simply walked out of their homes with only the clothes they were wearing and gathered at Hazbeger's house seeking transfer to the other estates.

When the final count was made, one thousand six hundred and sixty-six commanders in charge of nearly twelve billion angels were firmly committed to Lucifer. They were ready to renounce their loyalty to Almighty God, pledge themselves to Lucifer and make him their god.

Sixty-two commanders, leading more than four hundred and thirty million angels, prepared to leave their homes, their lands and their positions to seek safety and a new beginning in the other estates.

About seven million other angels forsook their commanders and fled to the homes of friends. They did so quickly and quietly in order to escape confinement and torture.

Hazbeger notified the other sixty-one commanders to bring their angels and the refugees to a meeting in the First Estate. They did so immediately, hoping that all of this would be resolved without too much conflict.

Almost four hundred and forty million angels swooped into the great valley that was an enormous parade ground. Here the angels of the First Estate practiced for those occasions when they would honor the Creator with spectacular displays of worship and adoration.

The field was so large that more than four hundred million angels occupied only a part of one corner. Other activities were taking place toward the center and at the other end.

A great platform had been constructed. It was about two hundred feet wide, sixty feet deep and twelve feet high. Chairs were placed on either side of the center that would seat forty angels. Steps on the right and left of center led up to the platform. There were steps at either end of the platform as well as steps at the rear.

The angels from the Third Estate arranged themselves in a wide semi-circle, fanning out from the front of the platform. Since the angels occupied only one corner of the field, the platform had been constructed facing out toward the edge of the property. The outside edge of the field sloped upward, providing a natural theater.

One might think that in a crowd of more than four hundred million, those at the back of that assembly would not be able to see or hear what was happening on the stage. Angels' eyes and ears are much superior to those of humans. They can see and hear quite clearly from a distance of several miles as easily as humans can from a hundred feet.

Suddenly, from behind those seated on the hillside came forty-two angels. They flew over the heads of the waiting assembly. Choosing not to use the steps, they settled gracefully onto the stage and all but two of them sat in the chairs provided.

Those two angels walked to the front of the platform and stood side by side about seven feet apart. The audience recognized them immediately---Michael and Gabriel. A roar of applause rose from the crowd. It was a shout of appreciation for what they anticipated those great angels would do for them. The applause subsided and a hush fell over the whole area. All ears listened to hear what would be said.

"Welcome to our estate," said Michael. "We didn't have

much time to prepare, so there are no pretty decorations. But, we have more important things to do here than enjoy a beautifully decorated platform.

"I want to give you my personal welcome and assure you that we will provide for your every need. The Creator Himself is very concerned about your well-being and has instructed us to take charge of transferring you into estates One and Two.

"The Creator asked me to convey His personal assurances to you that you have made the right choice and you will be blessed for choosing to seek His will when you were tempted to follow Lucifer. Gabriel will give you a few instructions now," said Michael.

Gabriel's voice filled the air with a soothing warmth that caused every angel to feel confident and eager to accomplish this transfer as soon as possible. "I was so pleased when the Almighty gave me this assignment with Michael," he said. "We brought forty commanders with us to help us handle the matter efficiently.

"Our commanders will spread out across the platform. We want every one of you commanders to come forward and speak with one of these. You will register with him and make an appointment to go to his office later with a complete list of the angels that came with you, including the refugees. More instructions will be given to you then."

Thirty-six of the commanders on the platform took their positions and began registering the sixty-two commanders that came from the Third Estate. The other four consulted with Gabriel and Michael concerning the next phase of integrating the millions of angels who had come to them.

"We don't have much time," said Michael. "We must not get too involved in property or career assignments."

"Why not?" asked Albamahn. "Don't we want to get

them fully integrated right away?"

Michael paused for a moment and then replied, "There is going to be a war."

"A war?" whispered Albamahn. "How do you know that? Surely this problem can be solved without a war."

Michael replied, "God knew what Lucifer would do before this evil plan ever entered his mind. However, God wants to give him every chance to stop. The punishment will be eternal and so severe for Lucifer and his followers that the rest of us will be deterred from even thinking of any future rebellion.

"Not only that, God is not willing that any of them should perish, but that they all should repent and stop this madness. God created them. He loves them. He does not want to see them plunge into eternal destruction.

"Lucifer has probably already made his eternal decision and so have the twelve billion angels who are rebelling with him. Only an all-out war will clarify it for all of us."

Michael continued, "I will keep all of you informed as things happen. Believe me, you will see how much God loves His creation and how it grieves Him to punish those made in His image. You will observe how we can use our freedom and power of choice to separate ourselves from our Creator.

"You will also see that God has no choice but to punish iniquity. Now, I'm not sure of all that this means, but He told me there is a vast difference between mistakes followed by sincere repentance and eternal rebellion.

"I have a feeling," Michael said, "that we are going to learn a great lesson about our relationship to Him who created us. Anyway, He told me that I must prepare the First Estate for war. He did not mention the Second Estate. I trust that God will give us everything we need to be victorious. I still wonder why He did not include the Second Estate.

"As I left the Throne-room I heard Him say, 'I can do with many or few.' With God Himself as our source of strength, we cannot fail.

"Well," concluded Michael, "I see they are finished registering the commanders. Let's go and get busy. We need to furnish temporary quarters for about four hundred and forty million guests."

Those angels assigned to the First Estate were shocked to learn that they would be immediately trained for battle. They believed, however, that they would be victorious.

The refugees assigned to the Second Estate were happy that they were not included in the preparations for war. They went forward with interviews and applications for their new positions.

An emergency call was sounded throughout the First and Second estates. Every angel was commanded to assemble in the immense area between the estates and the properties bordering the glassy sea in front of the Throne.

Michael and Gabriel were there. While the last angels were still arriving, Gabriel spoke loudly and briefly. "We are going immediately to the high mountain range overlooking the Third Estate. Michael and I want you to see what Lucifer and his followers have done. Quickly now, follow us."

As quickly as they could, more than twenty-four billion angels followed Michael and Gabriel. They spread out along the tops of the mountains and looked toward the Third Estate. They could not believe what their eyes saw.

The sixty-two whole areas of the commanders who had fled from Lucifer were totally destroyed. Smoke from raging fires rose high into the air. Other properties belonging to the seven million angels who had escaped from their commanders were also burning. The homes of the twelve generals and one hundred and forty-four captains were engulfed in flames. It was a scene that would never be forgotten.

Michael spoke. "This is what Lucifer has done in his hatred of those who refused to join in his rebellion. We must all realize the seriousness of this situation.

"I want all of us to meditate for a few moments on the difference between serving God and serving Lucifer. Lucifer is becoming a destroyer. He is in fact destroying himself and all those who chose to follow him.

"God, however, is patient and kind and loving. He desires only good for everyone He has created. God cannot, though, excuse Lucifer's rebellion. The time for judgment will come, but only after Lucifer has made his rebellion complete."

Michael continued, "I don't fully understand all of this and I don't know exactly what God will do. However, I am confident that He will not only execute justice, He will somehow also show mercy.

"Now, angels of the Second Estate, go back and continue your affairs. First Estate angels, we have been selected by heaven's Righteous Judge to assist Him in bringing Lucifer and his wicked plans to justice. Let's go!"

Chapter Four

Rebellion

"Gabriel, I want you to go to Lucifer and ask him to come and talk with Me." The words issued from the Throne with the pathos of a father seeking a straying son. "Speak kindly to him. I want him to know he is welcome here. I want him to know that I love him. I want him to know that I am concerned about him. I want him to know that he can talk with Me about anything---anything at all. Gabriel, be very gentle and kind to him."

"Yes Lord," replied Gabriel, "I shall do my best. I shall be gentle. However, may I make a request?"

God said, "Of course."

"Lord, please clothe me with Your protection. Also, please speak Your words through my mouth. I want Lucifer to sense Your love in my words. I don't want him to feel like I am confronting him."

The voice proceeding from the Throne sounded different this time. It was more than sad, it was broken. "Thank you, Gabriel, for seeking My heart. You just open your mouth and My Spirit will give you the words to say. I will protect you from harm."

Gabriel bowed down and backed slowly away. He did this voluntarily. He did it as an expression of gratitude for the many blessings God had given him. He did it to show his love for the One who had created him and fashioned him into the mighty angel that he is.

As he neared the attending angels who serve in the area

surrounding the Throne, he stood up straight and turned to depart. He stopped. What was that?

A sound echoed from the Throne, a sound that shocked all who heard it. The voice of God was sobbing, great heaving sobs, coming from a heart that was crushed with grief. Anguished moans and groans, wrenching cries of despair filled the Throne-room as Gabriel and the attending angels stood there in horrified amazement. God was crying!

"Lucifer, Lucifer," He wailed, "Oh, Lucifer, My precious one. Why? Why? Why?"

There was such pity and agonizing grief in those words that the angels sensed a finality in them. Marlfor, one of those standing close to Gabriel, asked, "Do you suppose Lucifer has hardened his heart to the point of no return?"

"Well," replied Gabriel, "God knows the end from the beginning. He certainly knows what Lucifer will do. I am sure God already knows what Lucifer's punishment will be. It sounds to me like God is suffering in advance the pain of what He must do to cleanse heaven of the iniquity that is rising in the Third Estate."

Enberdi spoke up. "I just cannot understand how one who is created in the image of God, one who is blessed with honor and privilege, can turn away from his Creator like that. Doesn't he realize what a terrible thing he is doing? And how can twelve billion angels be so dumb as to follow him in a plot that can only end in tragedy?"

Gabriel pondered those questions for a moment, then replied, "It was a long time ago, but I remember it well. I heard Erolhadmoran speaking at a convention. He is one of the commanders in the Third Estate who brought every one of his angels with him to escape from Lucifer.

"He said, 'Sin severs the optic nerve of the soul.' I never forgot those words. It seems to me that Lucifer has not only deceived twelve billion angels, he has deceived himself. Oh, how blind are those who refuse to see."

Ginrebbidor, who had been listening carefully, sighed and said, "I certainly hope Lucifer will listen to God and repent. What do you suppose will happen if he doesn't?"

Gabriel replied, "God told Michael to prepare all of the angels of the First Estate for war. I hope for the best, but I fear the worst may happen. However, it is my job right now to go and invite Lucifer to come and talk with God about all of this."

With that, he bade them goodbye and departed, heading toward the Third Estate and Lucifer's house. The Third Estate was as large as the entire surface of earth, including the oceans. Lucifer's mansion was located near the center.

Gabriel flew a circuitous route, sadly viewing at close range the destruction that had occurred there. Guards near the perimeter saw him and flew instantly to notify Lucifer.

Lucifer quickly went to his office and opened the closet door. He selected the most regal and official robe and dressed himself in it. He sat down at his desk, stiffened to his maximum height and waited.

Gabriel was ushered in by Timbedlar, the butler whom Lucifer had selected to replace Rowan. Gabriel noticed that Timbedlar bowed before Lucifer in much the same way he himself had bowed before God in heaven's Throne-room.

Lucifer sat there, stiff and glowering, not saying a word. It was an awkward moment.

Gabriel ignored the obvious air of tension in the room, put on his best smile and began to speak. "It has been such a long time since I have seen you. Let's see, when was it? Oh, yes, it was at the big celebration when all three estates got together. That surely was one to remember."

Lucifer stared disdainfully at Gabriel and did not speak. The brief silence was painful.

48

Gabriel breathed a silent prayer for God to help him. He smiled warmly and said, "I bring you greetings from the Creator. He asked me to invite you to the Throne-room. It seems you haven't talked with Him for quite a while. He would love to see you and talk with you."

"I am much too busy to talk with Him right now," snapped Lucifer. "You tell Him that I will talk with Him when I have a convenient time."

"Lucifer, please..." begged Gabriel.

"You heard what I said," roared Lucifer. "Now get out. Get out of here and don't you ever come into my house again. Timbedlar, show this slaving, obedient servant of God to the door. Then, be sure to wash his footsteps from our property."

Gabriel would have been embarrassed and humiliated, but he somehow felt the pain and grief of the Spirit of God within himself. He departed, walking some distance first, then rising above the houses and trees and flying. He looked back at the Third Estate and sadly wondered how this would end.

When Gabriel arrived at the outer court of the Throne-room he was met by Pladmordan the chief attending angel. "The Father thanks you for your efforts to invite Lucifer," he said. "God wants you to know that He appreciates your loyalty and faithfulness. Right now, He is so grief-stricken that He asks you to accept His thanks from me."

"You are very kind," replied Gabriel. "I shall return with a large group of angels to express our sympathy and to share in His grief."

"That is quite thoughtful of you," said Pladmordan, "but He requests that you wait until this matter is concluded and then organize both estates One and Two to appropriately grieve for the Third Estate."

Gabriel returned to his home and inquired of his assistants how the integration of the refugees was progressing.

Meanwhile, Michael was preparing the First Estate for war. Refugee angels from the Third Estate gave him information that was vital, should there be war.

The angels attending the entrance to the Throne-room were not allowing anyone to request an audience with the King. A pall of sadness was over the entire area. Even the various groups of praisers outside were touched by the grief inside.

Suddenly, a stir of excitement swept through the outer courts. One of the attending angels rushed to Pladmordan the chief officer and spoke in a loud whisper, "Lucifer is coming!"

"Get ready," was the instant reply. "We must not make any mistakes. Sintarbal, you accompany Lucifer from the outer court. Bergistamal, you join them at the circle. I will announce him without delay."

Lucifer was ushered into the presence of God in swift, but courteous fashion. He walked boldly up to the Throne, dressed in his most impressive uniform. He stood arrogantly stiff. He did not bow.

"Welcome," said the Father, "it has been such a long time. I have missed you so much and have longed to see you. I remember the long talks we used to have and I do so hope that we can walk together in the gardens again like we used to."

Lucifer interrupted most rudely, "I have no time for such things anymore. I just came to tell You that I am breaking away and forming my own kingdom."

A crowd of angels had gathered as near as possible in the inner court. They listened breathlessly to what was being said.

The Father spoke gently, "Lucifer, please don't do this. My heart is broken at the very thought of what you are planning. Already you have destroyed much and have caused great harm among the angels. Please change your mind. Please come back to Me.

"There can only be one God. Anything else results in chaos. I cannot permit you to do this thing. You are destroying yourself and you are leading billions of others to destruction with you.

"Don't you see what you are doing? Please come back to Me. Repent of those evil intentions. Submit to My rule. I will forgive you of everything. I will restore everything, only please don't continue down the pathway of evil. It can only end in tragedy for you and for those who follow you.

"Lucifer, remember that although I am a forgiving Father, I am also a just Judge. Please don't force Me to judge you. Cast that pride out of your heart and humble yourself." Streams of tears were flowing down the Father's face. His voice was broken and pleading.

Lucifer stood there silent for a long moment. He relaxed just a bit and seemed to be in deep thought.

The listening angels whispered among themselves, "What will he say? What will he do? Surely he will not continue this madness. Surely he will come to his senses and realize that he has made a terrible mistake. Surely he will respond to the heartfelt pleading of the Father."

Lucifer stiffened again. The angels stopped their whispers. All ears listened intently, hoping to hear the best.

Moving backward one step and slightly toward his right, Lucifer turned his head and glared straight at the Throne. "I have gone too far," he said. "My mind is made up. No one can stop me now, not even You. I have twelve billion angels committed to my cause and they are ready to fight.

They will destroy anyone who tries to stop us."

He turned his back and started to walk away. Then suddenly, he whirled around, pointed his finger straight at the Throne and shouted, "Your sad words and Your phony tears don't fool me. You just can't stand for anyone else to rule, can You? I will never reach my full potential as long as I keep bowing down and submitting to rules and regulations designed only to praise and glorify You.

"I shall build my own kingdom, thank You, and I shall rule it my way. At last, I shall receive the honor I deserve." Turning again, Lucifer stormed out, shouting at the listening angels, "What are you staring at, you bunch of spineless wimps."

Silence, you could almost feel it. There was only the sound of angry footsteps fading into the distance, then nothing. No sound came from the Throne. The golden glow that continually filled the whole area dimmed for a moment.

The angels remained motionless, their minds in utter shock at what had just happened. Now what? How could Lucifer, so greatly honored and blessed with such high and holy position, do such a thing? How could a created being of any rank dare talk to his Creator like that?

Lucifer flew over the areas where his angels had destroyed his enemies' houses and lands. He obtained a grim satisfaction viewing the smoldering remains. He knew he could do it. He knew what the first campaign would be.

No more planning, no more delay. He moved quickly to his house and called for Milnahtan, Ginzbarel and Yenthapen to come to his office immediately. They flew in almost together. Timbedlar ushered them with instructions to bow completely down on the floor and begin calling Lucifer "Master."

They did so, lying face down on the floor at a distance of about fifteen feet, saying "Master, Master, Master." They stayed there on the floor until Lucifer told them to stand up.

"It is time to fight," he said. "I have seen the other two estates and it is obvious that the Second Estate is not making any plans for war at all. They are going about their business as usual. Stupid idiots.

"The First Estate is making some preparations but they will be no match for us with our superior training.

"Now, here is what we will do. First, we will attack the Second Estate. Nobody expects us to do that. With them conquered, the First Estate will have no one to help them. This is going to be much easier than I thought.

"Do you three generals know what this means? Yes, I am promoting you to the rank of general. This means we will have it all. Think of it. We will rule all of creation.

"Aren't you glad you decided to obey me? Aren't you glad you are not over there with those traitors? Just wait until we get our hands on them. Oh, how they will suffer. What tortures I will think of to torment them with. I will be the god of all creation and you will help me rule it.

"Go now, get your commanders in order. Tell them to get their troops ready for war. We must move immediately. The element of surprise is vital. The three of you, meet me at the perimeter near the high mountains. I will give you further instructions there. Go quickly now. There is not a moment to lose."

The three new generals flew off together, congratulating each other on their promotions. "Lucifer sure delivers on his promises, doesn't he?" exclaimed Milnahten.

"Yes, he does," said Ginzbarel. "I wonder what our next promotion will be? Is there anything above general?"

Yenthapen calmed their excitement with, "We have to win this thing first. I can't believe it is going to be as easy as Lucifer says it is. Let's just give the commanders hard, crisp orders and go out to the battle as if it is going to be a tough fight. Let's not take anything for granted."

Chapter Five

Attack

Mendenalboral was one of the lookouts stationed on the peaks of the mountains overlooking the Third Estate. His job was to notify Marlann, a high-ranking commander in the Second Estate, if he saw any suspicious activity. He had seen Lucifer going back home after his meeting with God and was now especially watchful.

Suddenly he saw vast numbers of Lucifer's troops advancing. They were still thousands of miles away but they were moving rapidly.

Swifter than an eagle he flew straight to the Second Estate. He landed at the front door of Marlann's mansion. The butler had been instructed to escort him into the office immediately upon his arrival.

The door opened almost as soon as he rang the golden bell. Genridday the butler rushed him to Marlann's office.

"Come in," said Marlann, rising from his desk and walking to meet him. "What news do you have?"

"They are coming," announced Mendenalboral. "They are heading right here for the Second Estate. Why would they do that? We have not made any preparations to fight."

Marlann replied, "That is exactly why they are attacking us first."

"But we've never done anything to harm them," objected Mendenalboral.

"They want to capture and enslave us," said Marlann. "Then they will attack the First Estate."

Mendenalboral thought for a moment and then said, "If

they want to have their own kingdom, why don't they just declare their independence? Why do they have to fight against us? We are not their enemies."

Marlann lifted the palms of his hands outward, shrugged his shoulders and said, "I don't know. Maybe Lucifer thinks he can depose God and rule over all creation."

Marlann placed his right elbow into his left hand, circled his chin with his right thumb and forefinger, pursed his lips and moved his head slowly from side to side. Then he spoke. "You know, Mendy, when a person turns against the One who created him, something must be terribly wrong with his thinking. Perhaps pride has festered in his heart until he has become completely paranoid."

"What is 'paranoid'?" asked Mendenalboral.

"Well," said Marlann thoughtfully, "I once took a class on how to think good thoughts. Descriptions of some bad thoughts were given to contrast them with good thoughts. Pride was explained as the basic sin underlying all other thinking that takes us out of harmony with our Creator.

"The professor said that pride, left unchecked, could lead a person to paranoia, which is an exaggerated sense of one's own importance, with a dark distrust and suspicion of other people and their motives.

"In the most extreme case," continued Marlann, "it could cause one's thinking patterns to actually reverse. A person might become so twisted in his thinking that he would call good 'evil' and call evil 'good.'

"If that be the case, then Lucifer considers us to be his enemies, roadblocks to be overcome if he is to achieve his goals. Mendy, don't ever think more highly of yourself than you ought. You may work hard for promotion, but don't ever let it plant the seeds of pride in your heart."

Mendy, as Marlann called him, responded, "Are we just

going to stand here and let them overwhelm us?"

Marlann quickly replied, "Just before you arrived, I received orders from headquarters. The orders read, 'Be calm and be assured that I am God and I will protect you.'

"I asked the messenger what that meant. He smiled and replied, 'The Lord is my strength and my shield. I shall not be afraid.' He then turned and left without another word. I take that to mean we will be protected somehow."

Mendy began pacing back and forth. "Well," he said, "I think we ought to do something."

"I'll tell you what," announced Marlann, "I'll get the butler and a few officers together and we'll go to the perimeter and watch what happens. Come on, let's go."

Away they all went, joining a host of others who were gathering to watch the oncoming horde of warriors from the Third Estate.

The sky was filled with them, twelve billion highly trained and equipped soldiers, flying headlong to meet with destiny. As they approached the perimeter, they increased their speed, faster and faster they flew, the front ranks rushing ahead.

Suddenly, the front ranks crashed into something, an invisible wall of some kind. They were crushed by millions of troops smashing into them from behind. They slid down the invisible wall, smearing their bodies to the ground. By observing the smears, one could, in a sense, "see" the wall.

By the time the rushing hordes could stop, one hundred and eighty-five million angels had crashed or been pushed into that invisible wall. They lay in great heaps of smashed and mangled bodies on the ground.

Marlann and Mendy were watching the catastrophic event from inside the wall. Endigreber, a commander who lived near Marlann, was discussing this unexpected defense with them.

"I know a commander," he said, "whose captain attended a high level meeting some time ago. He told me that God Himself was the main speaker. During the speech God was talking about possible future events and how He is available to help us when we need Him.

"He tried to quote the exact words God said. They were something like this. 'In her time of trouble I will be a wall around her and My glory will be in her midst.' God certainly has provided this wall of protection here for us." They turned around and looked behind them. The glow of light in the air was shining more brightly.

On the other side of that invisible wall, Lucifer was trying to keep his troops from complete panic. He flew over them, shouting orders to the commanders. They were rushing around on the ground, gazing at the bodies of their comrades and wondering what to do next.

Lucifer gathered his three generals and several top commanders together and conferred with them. Milnahten spoke up and said to Lucifer, "I thought you said this was going to be easy. Look what happened. Have you got any more surprises for us?"

"Shut up!" shouted Lucifer. "This is no time to be pointing fingers. We have to get inside that wall."

Ginzbarel suggested, "Maybe it is only so high. Perhaps we can fly over it."

"You idiot," snarled Lucifer. "Whoever put it there surely knows we could fly over the top of a wall. That thing is probably like a dome over the whole Second Estate. No, we've got to find a way through it."

Yenthapen said, "Master, let me go examine that wall and see what I can find. Perhaps I can discover something."

"That is the first intelligent thing I have heard here," replied Lucifer. "Go and see what you can do."

Yenthapen went to the wall, walking on top of the piles of bodies lying there. He walked along pounding with his fist on the wall. He saw angels of the Second Estate on the other side staring at him and the millions of bodies.

Coming to a place where the bodies were not piled so high against the wall, he stopped and shouted, "Hello there, what is your name? You, with the blue belt, come here."

The angel with the blue belt stepped over to the wall. "My name is Fredmorgan," he replied. "What is yours?"

"I am Yenthapen. Can you knock on the wall like this?" he asked, pounding on the invisible wall.

Fredmorgan put his fist forward and it went right through the wall.

"Try putting your foot through," said Yenthapen.

Fredmorgan pushed his foot through the wall and drew it back. "Wow!" he said, "this is a one-way wall. We can go through it but you cannot come in."

"Exactly," said Yenthapen. "I need your help."

"What do you mean?" asked Fredmorgan.

"Let me explain," replied Yenthapen. "You see, we need to talk. This whole matter can be resolved peacefully if we can just talk.

"Lucifer does not want any more destruction. He wants to discuss with your leaders how it may be settled wisely and well. We were not coming to attack you. We just wanted to talk with you about our plans.

"Now, look what has happened. Don't you see how unreasonable the Almighty One is? He has erected an invisible wall here and has crushed millions of precious angels that He Himself created.

"What do you think He will do to you if you make a

mistake? He is not a loving God. He is angry and hate-filled. He is waiting for all of you to slip just a little so He can vent His wrath on you. Listen to me, Fredmorgan, you can be the one who spares us all from more destruction.

"Please, Fredmorgan, come through the wall. I will personally escort you to Lucifer. He will give you a message of peace to deliver to your leaders. You will be a hero. Believe me, Fredmorgan, this is the only way. Come on, step through the wall. I will personally see that you are rewarded greatly for your wisdom and heroism."

Fredmorgan stepped through the wall and accompanied Yenthapen to the command station where Lucifer was in conference with several commanders.

"Look what I have," announced Yenthapen, "a hostage."

"But you said…" interrupted Fredmorgan.

"Shut up, you stupid jerk," shouted Yenthapen. "Take him away and torture him," he barked at the nearby guards.

"Well," smirked Lucifer, "I have one general I can depend on. Tell me, what do you suggest next?"

Yenthapen's thoughts quickly organized as to just how to answer his dangerous and paranoid leader.

Bowing low and remaining there until Lucifer bade him rise, he demonstrated to all those present his absolute submission to Lucifer. Then he spoke. "Master, let me submit my humble plan for your consideration. Your wisdom will quickly discern if it is worthy.

"Let us inform our enemies that we have a hostage. Let us tell them of his pain and torture. Let us plead with them to end his suffering by agreeing to send a delegation of top officials to meet with us and discuss how we might together find an appropriate solution to this difficult situation in which we all find ourselves."

Lucifer's shrewd mind was already on top of that

proposal. "Yenthapen," he said, "do you really think those leaders will come here and listen to us and then go back and cooperate with us in the overthrow of their own government? Come on, they can't be that dumb."

Yenthapen quickly replied, "Getting them here is only the beginning of our strategy. This poor soul I tricked into coming here will arouse their concern for his safety. Their compassion for him just might motivate them to send important angels into our midst. Then, we will have high level hostages and can force them to accept our terms."

"What if your plan doesn't work?" queried Lucifer.

"In that case," responded Yenthapen, "we haven't gained anything, but we haven't lost anything either. If it doesn't work, we will devise another plan. Let's try this plan first. If it fails, I am ready to hear other suggestions."

"All right," said Lucifer, "I am putting you in charge of it and I am holding you responsible to make it work." With that, Lucifer rose and walked away to assure his commanders and their troops that success and victory would soon be realized.

Yenthapen discussed with several commanders in his area how they might proceed. They decided to send an unimportant angel with the offer to talk, just in case he might be held hostage like they were holding Fredmorgan.

"But how will he get through the wall?" asked one of the commanders.

"I don't know," replied Yenthapen. "Maybe he will just talk through the wall and someone inside will deliver the message to their leaders. Anyway, he is expendable. We are not as compassionate as they are. We will sacrifice as many of our troops as we must in order to attain our goal."

Chapter Six

Defeat

Daplendar reported to Marlann that Fredmorgan had gone with Yenthapen to Lucifer's camp.

"That was a bad mistake," sighed Marlann. "He shouldn't have done that. It is almost certain they will hold him hostage in an effort to force us to accommodate them in some way."

Just then, Genridday rushed in and announced, "An angel from the Third Estate is here. It seems he tunneled under the invisible wall. He says he has a message. Do you wish to speak to him?"

"Yes, bring him in," answered Marlann. The visitor was ushered into the office. He bowed low to the floor and remained there.

"Please stand up sir," said Marlann in a kind and gentle voice. "I want you to meet my chief butler, Genridday. Also, please meet my friend Mendenalboral. We call him 'Mendy' for short. These others are members of my staff who help me administrate my area of command.

"Sir, you look tired. Please sit down," invited Marlann. Everyone sat down and made themselves comfortable.

Marlann turned to Genridday and said, "Please ask someone to bring us something refreshing to drink."

Genridday left the room briefly and then returned. Almost immediately, trays laden with glasses of cool purple liquid arrived and were distributed.

Looking pleasantly at his guest and smiling, Marlann inquired, "Sir, what is your name?"

"Thomlin," was the reply.

"And what can we do for you?" continued Marlann.

"They sent me with a message, not a very nice message, I'm afraid," answered Thomlin. "They have one of your angels named Fredmorgan. They are torturing him mercilessly. They are demanding that your leaders send a delegation to talk with them. They say they will release Fredmorgan as soon as your delegation arrives."

"Do you know what they want to talk with us about?" asked Marlann.

Thomlin replied, "They say they want to work out an arrangement to settle this matter peacefully without any further destruction and harm."

Marlann looked about the room for a moment and then asked a question intended for everyone present, "Are you thinking what I'm thinking?"

"We certainly are," said Mendy. "They will capture those important leaders and hold them hostage also. They will then pressure us to meet their demands in order to secure the release of the hostages."

Marlann shifted in his chair, leaned forward over his desk and spoke slowly. "We care deeply about Fredmorgan. We want him brought back safely to us. However, are we willing to risk several of our leaders, maybe even the security and future of our estate, on the mere chance they will honor their word and release him?"

"Fredmorgan has made a terrible mistake. We must not make an even greater mistake in our efforts to rescue him. As soon as we finish talking with Thomlin, I will contact Gabriel and see what he wants to do."

Thomlin slipped out of his chair and dropped to his knees on the floor. "Please sir," he begged, "don't send me back to them. Some of our angels came to you and you took them in. Could you please rescue me from Lucifer? I beg you, please."

Marlann stood up, walked around the desk, held out his hands and lifted Thomlin to his feet. His voice was soft and kind, but with a gentle ring of authority as he spoke. "Thomlin, you don't have to bow to me. You don't have to get on your knees before me."

He put his arms around Thomlin, hugged him warmly and said, "You are free to stay or go, whatever you wish. I can keep you here or I can ask one of the other commanders to let you join his people."

"Oh, please, please let me stay with you," begged Thomlin. "I'll scrub your floors. I'll do anything."

"Now, now, I'm sure we can find a better job for you than that," replied Marlann. "However, when I get back, you and I must have a serious talk.

"What the angels of the Third Estate have done is a terrible thing. Almighty God is not only a loving and wonderful Creator, He is also a just and righteous Judge. They have sinned and sin must be punished."

Thomlin cried, "What do you think He will do to me?"

"I don't know," replied Marlann. "I do know He loves you. If you are truly sorry for what has happened and sincerely desire to escape from Lucifer, maybe there is hope. If you throw yourself down before God and ask for mercy, He may possibly find a way to judge you with both justice and mercy.

"I have no idea how God can be true to His own nature as a Holy God to execute justice and still be merciful. I just don't know how He can do it. But if there is a way, I am confident He will do it. He created you. He loves you and He doesn't want to destroy you."

Marlann continued, "If God does find a way, I will be

happy to give you a place in my district. As a matter of fact, I need another angel to run errands and deliver messages for me. You could live here in the mansion and work for me. Would you like that?"

"Oh, that would be wonderful!" exclaimed Thomlin. "Will you help me?"

"There is really nothing I can do to help you," replied Marlann. "It is a personal matter between you and your Creator. There is nothing I or any other angel can do to satisfy God's holiness and justice for you.

"Well, I must go now," said Marlann. "I must see Gabriel as soon as possible. Oh, Genridday, will you ask someone to make our guest comfortable while I am gone? Please see that he is refreshed and ready to talk with me when I return."

Marlann lifted a folder out of a large file cabinet near his desk, put it into a briefcase and departed.

Genridday asked Mehrindal to accommodate Thomlin and then began discussing and comparing schedules with Stahrborni, Marlann's Chief of Staff.

Meanwhile, Lucifer and his generals were watching the wall closely to see if Thomlin would come back with any information. As they sat there in the command post discussing what to do next, Ginzbarel asked, "What can we do about the bodies piled up by that wall?"

"I'm not concerned about them," growled Lucifer. "They are of no use to us now. Ginzbarel, you and Milnahten go check on the commanders. See to it that they keep their troops under control. We must be ready to move immediately when I give the order. Yenthapen, you stay here with me."

Just then, Ginzbarel saw a well-armed soldier standing near the wall, staring at them. "Look," he said, "that looks like a soldier from the First Estate."

"Get over there and bring him to me," barked Lucifer. "We have ourselves another hostage."

Milnahten and Ginzbarel approached the angel and greeted him, while a host of soldiers surrounded him with swords drawn. "Hello," said Milnahten. "My name is Milnahten and this is Ginzbarel. What is your name?"

"I am Pallicahndar," he stated, "Commander of the Seventh District, in Section Eight, of the Fourth Division, in the First Estate. I want you to know exactly who I am and that I represent Michael the Archangel."

Ginzbarel and Milnahten looked at each other and snickered. Shaking his head in disgust, Ginzbarel sneered, "We are generals and Michael sent one lowly district commander to talk with us?"

Pallicahndar smiled. It was a rather sad smile, one filled with pity and compassion, yet a smile that indicated a quiet confidence. It would soon become evident that God empowers ordinary people to do extraordinary things.

Looking about at the soldiers with drawn swords, Pallicahndar then turned and faced the two generals. Humility, sadness and pity sounded in his voice as he spoke. "Gentlemen, you will remember my name throughout eternity and you will also remember these words---Almighty God will give great strength to His people and He will bless them with victory and peace.

"Milnahten and Ginzbarel, you are about to be disembodied." He drew his sword and held it high above his head. It began to glow with divine light that could only come directly from the Throne of the Creator.

The two generals leaped backwards, drew their swords and shouted to the soldiers, "Attack!" They moved back so the soldiers could completely surround Pallicahndar.

Something like a laser beam or death ray proceeded forth from his great sword. As he swung the sword round and round, hundreds of soldiers were literally cut in half. They fell to the ground mortally wounded.

Pouring from their awesome wounds was something that resembled blood, although of a much lighter color. Their spirits rose from their slaughtered bodies and hovered helplessly above. Within moments, more that a thousand angel bodies lay massacred around Pallicahndar.

Leaping over them and charging up to Milnahten and Ginzbarel, he raised his sword and prepared to strike. Both of them dropped to their knees and begged for mercy. One great stroke of that awesome sword separated their spirits from their bodies and sent them to join the others that were circling above.

Multitudes of Third Estate soldiers looked in horrified wonder at the mutilated corpses of their comrades. They viewed with amazement their spirits in the air above, now helpless to continue the battle. They stood back some distance. They did not want to share the fate of those who had fallen.

Suddenly, another angel came flying in high and from the direction of the First Estate. He dropped swiftly to the ground a short distance from Pallicahndar.

He was not nearly so humble and soft-spoken as Pallicahndar. He stood atop a small hill and shouted with a voice that reverberated throughout the camp. "I am Harmegiddown, your rendezvous with judgment. I come to you in the name of the Most High God. Judgment has come to you.

"Come to me. Come to me now," he roared. My sword will send you to stand before the Great Judge. Justice will be done. Come! Come!"

Not one soldier moved toward Harmegiddown. All was quiet. Then Lucifer rose into the air and shouted, "Attack him. Are you going to let one angel make cowards of all of you? He cannot possible defeat twelve billion soldiers. You will defeat him. Attack! Attack!"

Millions of troops rose up around Lucifer. Yenthapen moved close to him and said, "You lead us, Lucifer. With you leading us we cannot fail."

Lucifer replied, "No, my general, you lead them. I will supervise the battle from up here. Go now, win this battle for me."

Like an angry cloud they swirled above Harmegiddown. Then, like a tornado dropping from the sky, they funneled downward, completely blocking Lucifer's view.

Explosions of power erupted from the ground. Pieces of bodies were hurled outward from the swirling vortex. Piles of mangled soldiers began to form. Spirits torn from their bodies fluttered upward, gathering in clusters to watch the terrible scene.

Lucifer watched in dismay as millions of his troops were devastated by the awesome sword of Harmegiddown. "Crush him. Crush him," he screamed. "Attack! Attack! Crush him, you idiots, crush him."

A messenger from the rear flew breathlessly to Lucifer. "Master, Master," he gasped, "come and look."

Lucifer flew with him to a vantage point overlooking the whole area. He could not believe what he saw. Standing out there in full battle array was the entire army of the First Estate, twelve billion soldiers ready to fight. The archangel Michael stood at the forefront of that mighty force.

"It's all over, Master," said the messenger, "we're finished."

"Shut up, you fool," shouted Lucifer. He flew swiftly

back and forth, screaming at the commanders. "Attack, you fools, attack. Strike them down for me. Do it for me. Attack! Attack!"

Swarms of desperate troops rose into the air and flew headlong into the waiting army. The soldiers of the First Estate retreated rapidly in the center, farther and farther until a great many of Lucifer's troops were surrounded.

Suddenly, the retreating angels stopped and turned. They drew their swords. Every sword began to glow with the fire of God. Deadly beams issued forth from each one.

With a roar, the First Estate army attacked. Within minutes, more than two billion of Lucifer's troops lay vanquished before him. Then, almost ten billion soldiers threw down their swords and surrendered. Lucifer was defeated. The battle was over.

Michael flew to a hill not far from where Lucifer was flying about. "Come down here," commanded Michael. Lucifer circled for a moment, then landed on top of the hill, facing Michael.

"I am taking you to the Throne-room for judgment," said the archangel.

"Oh, no you're not," shouted Lucifer, drawing his sword. He brandished his weapon and snarled, "You're not dealing with an ordinary angel now. I am Lucifer the invincible. Draw your sword if you dare."

Michael stood there with his hands at his side. He looked with tender concern upon his opponent. "Come on, Lucifer, surrender quietly."

"Surrender? Did you say 'surrender'? I will never surrender, never." He gripped the handle of his sword in both hands and swung with all his might.

An invisible shield was around Michael. Lucifer's sword struck it and shattered into several pieces.

Michael reached out and took hold of Lucifer's arm in a grip that was stronger than a steel vise. He flew away, dragging Lucifer along screaming, "No! No! No!"

Chapter Seven

Prisoners

Michael took Lucifer to a place near the outer court of the Throne-room and bound him there with a chain that had the appearance of gold. It seemed almost like liquid gold, shining brilliantly. It was also very hot, for when Michael bound him with it, Lucifer screamed in agony. It burned through his clothing and seared his flesh.

An aide asked Michael what should be done with the defeated army of the Third Estate. He replied, "Bind them all and assemble them somewhere near here. Round up the spirits of the fallen ones also. Find Ehmlar and ask him to come here immediately. I have some special instructions for him."

The aide departed and Michael positioned himself to guard his prisoner.

"You'll never get away with this," snarled Lucifer, white froth forming at the edges of his mouth. "I shall escape and you will pay dearly."

Michael did not answer. Now that Lucifer was captured, there was really no reason to speak or act violently toward him. Michael watched his prisoner carefully and he grieved that so high an angel had fallen so far.

Ehmlar arrived and reported at once. Michael asked how things were going at the battlefield. "Most of our troops are binding the ten billion soldiers who surrendered," said Ehmlar. "Some are out gathering up the spirits of the slain. They have discovered that the power beams in their swords are as effective against spirits as they are against physical bodies."

"Very good," replied Michael. "Now, I have a special task for you. I want you to select about a thousand soldiers and go to the Third Estate. Search it to see if any of Lucifer's angels are hiding there. Keep all you find separate and bring them here to me."

Ehmlar departed and went immediately to his task. A thousand volunteers were quickly assembled and led to the Third Estate.

"How can one thousand of us possibly do this job quickly?" inquired Remzelad. "The Third Estate is so large. We need more angels to help us."

Ehmlar replied, "On my way to enlist you I questioned in my own mind why Michael had instructed me to take only about one thousand troops. I was suddenly given an answer directly from the Spirit of God. I am to wave my right hand over you and you will temporarily receive the ability to see through walls and buildings. You will be able to see anyone hiding, no matter where they are."

"But," objected Remzelad, "wouldn't it have been simpler to give us a million troops?"

Ehmlar thought for a moment and then answered, "I suppose we should just let God do things His way. It never hurts for us to ask questions, but we should be willing to submit to His will. I could have enlisted a million, but Michael told me to enlist a thousand. We may never have it explained to us, but it is better to obey than disobey. Let's do it His way."

Bergetman asked, "Are you going to wave your hand over each one of us?"

"I was not given that bit of information," said Ehmlar, "so I choose to wave my hand over all of you at once. Hey! Everyone, look up here."

He waved his hand from side to side over the thousand

angels as they gazed at him. They didn't feel any different. They looked about and did not see things differently. However, they would soon discover that as they needed that power, it would enable them to see through walls and buildings and find those who were hiding.

Ehmlar organized them and laid out their flight paths for them. He then sent them on their ways with instructions to bring all those whom they found back to him unharmed, if possible.

Away they went in teams of two, spreading out in precise flight paths designed to assure complete coverage of the Third Estate.

Marlow and Ebzgon were together, flying through the center of the Third Estate, looking to the left and to the right as they flew. They noticed that they were covering a great amount of territory rather quickly.

Suddenly, Marlow spotted something. "Look Ebzgon, down there inside that building. Do you see what I see?"

"Let's go down there," replied Ebzgon. "Get your sword ready, just in case." They flew swiftly downward and landed near the front door of a very large mansion.

"This looks like the home of a commander," said Marlow. "Let's be careful."

They stepped cautiously inside and looked about, their swords drawn. For some reason their swords did not begin glowing this time. They wondered about that and what it might mean.

As they carefully searched each room on either side of the long hallway, they noticed a white piece of cloth waving from a slightly opened door.

Cautiously approaching, they demanded, "Open up and surrender." The door opened to reveal a commander holding the white cloth. He unbuckled his sword and let it fall to the floor. Behind him stood six of his personal staff. They dropped their swords also.

Marlow asked in a gentle tone, "Who are you?"

"I am Thergalozar, Commander of this district," he said.

"Do not be afraid," said Marlow. "We will not harm anyone who surrenders peacefully. Are these few angels all that remain in your district?"

Thergalozar explained, "Some of my people panicked and escaped to the First Estate. Most of my seven million angels went with Lucifer. My close staff members here and I discussed our concerns about Lucifer's plan and decided to hide for a while and then see if we could get to the First Estate without being caught by Lucifer."

"It was wise to make that decision," remarked Ebzgon.

The commander asked, "What will you do with us?"

"Our orders," replied Marlow, "are to take you to Michael, the Archangel of the First Estate. That is all we know at this point." Then he continued, "We must bind you so you cannot escape, but we will not harm you."

Ebzgon and Marlow took their prisoners and continued the search. In a surprisingly short time, all of the Third Estate angels who had not accompanied Lucifer were rounded up and brought to Ehmlar, then led in one large group to Michael, as he had requested.

They were registered by name in a separate register and placed in a camp apart from all the others. They numbered twenty-four thousand nine hundred and fifty-two.

The archangel walked into their midst to talk with them. "I am Michael," he said. "I welcome you here and I have sent for refreshments for you. We will make your brief stay in this place as comfortable as possible. We will not harm you unless you try to escape. We are simply holding you here until the Almighty Himself will judge you.

"Now," continued Michael, "let me ask you a question. Why did you not accompany Lucifer to the battle?"

Rhintusperel, a lieutenant in the Third Estate, stepped forward. "Please let me speak," he said. "I can probably answer for everyone."

He explained, "Some of us individually and some of us in small groups decided that we had made a terrible mistake in remaining with Lucifer. We concluded that what he is doing is wrong. We also realized that if he is successful he will punish us horribly.

"We decided, however, to stand for what is right, regardless of the consequences. Now, we may appear to you as being cowardly, but we did the best we knew how under the circumstances. We realize that we got ourselves into a situation from which there is no easy way out."

Rhintusperel continued, "I really think I am speaking the hearts and minds of all these, my fellow prisoners. We decided that it would be better to throw ourselves down before the merciful and loving God who created us, than follow the wicked schemes of a merciless traitor."

He concluded by saying, "If we seem to just be seeking the easy way out of our dilemma, well, maybe we are, but what else can we do? We admit our wrong and ask for mercy. Will you help us, please?"

Michael replied, "The only help I can give you is to keep you safe and comfortable here until I deliver you to the Throne-room for judgment. Your future is between you and your Creator. He is your Judge. I cannot appeal to Him on your behalf. You must, each one of you, stand before Him to be judged for what you have done.

"I have no idea what your judgment will be. I wish I could be more encouraging, but I really don't know what our Almighty Judge will do with you."

Michael paused for a moment. Tears formed in his eyes. They overflowed and ran down his cheeks. He cleared his throat and continued in a trembling voice. "I was standing in the inner court when Lucifer issued his final words of rebellion. After he left, I heard God weeping over His lost child. I am sure that God grieves over you also.

"I'm sorry," sobbed Michael, "I'm so sorry. Please refresh yourselves and be as comfortable as you can while we wait for God's judgment in this matter."

Just then, Girthimly, the aide whom Michael had sent with instructions concerning the Third Estate army, arrived and reported. "The prisoners have all been bound," he said. "We have selected the large area beyond the plain that borders the outer courts.

"With your permission," he continued, "we will begin assembling them by divisions there. Also, with your permission, we will ask the library to loan us the official register of the Third Estate, so that every name may be accounted for and the official disposition of each of the prisoners recorded."

"Very good," replied Michael. "That is a good plan. Please keep me advised as to how it is going and please let me know if any problems develop."

Girthimly said, "I see Lucifer sitting over there. Has he given you any trouble?"

"No," answered Michael. "He made a few threats, but mostly he has just been sitting there talking to himself."

"What about those prisoners over there? Where did they come from?" inquired Girthimly.

Michael explained, "Ehmlar took some troops and found them hiding in the Third Estate. We will deliver them as a separate group for judgment."

Girthimly departed, promising to further advise Michael

about the assembling of the prisoners. Arriving at the battlefield, he informed the division generals that Michael approved their plans for an orderly accounting.

Girthimly asked for a contingent of angels to carry the registration books from the library to the assembly area.

Marzteblar, General of the Fourth Division, suggested that angels from the Second Estate be asked to do that job. "We should let them share in what we are doing," he said.

"Oh, by the way, Girthimly," inquired Marzteblar, "do you know if that invisible wall is still there?"

"I'll find out on my way to the Second Estate," answered Girthimly. "I'm sure it isn't needed anymore."

"Well, don't bump into it," cautioned Marzteblar with a grin that stretched across his bronzed face.

Girthimly chuckled and replied, "I think I can pass right through it. However, I'll be careful."

He rose into the air and flew away to see Marlann, his friend in the Second Estate.

Chapter Eight

Judgment

Girthimly arrived at Marlann's mansion and was ushered into the large office by Genridday, the butler.

Marlann greeted him warmly and inquired, "Is the invisible wall still there?"

"Yes," he answered, "I went up close and could still see the smears. It is still there."

"Praise God!" exclaimed Marlann. "Our God truly is a shield and a wall of protection around us. We must plan a celebration of thanksgiving for His wonderful care."

"That is a good idea," responded Girthimly. "However, right now I have a favor to ask. Would you send some of your angels with me to the library to carry the Third Estate register books to the assembly area where the prisoners are being gathered?"

"Of course," said Marlann. "How many angels do you think you need?"

"Well," replied Girthimly, "there are more than twelve billion names recorded in the Third Estate. That's a lot of books to carry."

"I'll ask five hundred volunteers to go with you," said Marlann. "If you need more, just ask."

Girthimly smiled and said, "Thank you. I think five hundred will be sufficient."

Marlann suggested, "Please go and wait at the intersection of Floral Avenue and Pearl Street, near Berbelan's house. They will meet you there."

Girthimly departed and walked the short distance to the

appointed place. Berbelan came out of his house and said, "Hello there, may I help you?"

"No, I'm just waiting for some people," he replied. "I am Girthimly from the First Estate. I have some volunteers coming to help me carry books from the library. We need to record all of the prisoners of the Third Estate."

Berbelan commented, "That will be a big job."

"Yes," responded Girthimly, "it sure will. Oh, look, here come my helpers now."

The five hundred angels flew off with Girthimly to the library. As the books were checked out to them, it became evident that more help was needed. An angel named Pherredi flew back and enlisted another hundred volunteers to help carry the books.

The journey took longer than anticipated because of the weight of the thousands of volumes.

One by one the divisions of the Third Estate had been brought to the designated area. They were shackled in groups of one hundred, but their hands were left free to receive the food provided.

Girthimly and his helpers arrived with the books and presented them to the generals. An orderly count was made to be sure each of Lucifer's dedicated followers was listed for judgment.

The names of the defectors from the Third Estate were extracted and written separately so they could be compared with the lists registered in the First and Second estates.

All of the captives found hiding in the Third Estate were listed and kept separate from the other prisoners.

When the accounting was finished, Girthimly asked Benhalowmar, the officer in charge of the registration, if the books were ready to be returned to the library.

"No," he replied, "we must mark the permanent record

of each one as to his judgment and his change of location. We must be able to inquire of the library about any angel and find his current status and location. That may seem unnecessary right now, but it could be very useful two or three billion years from now in history classes."

Word came from the Throne-room that Lucifer, his commanders and lieutenants were to be brought in as soon as possible for judgment.

Lieutenants of the First Estate were left in charge of the prisoners so the commanders, captains, generals and archangels could personally witness the judgment of the Third Estate.

Michael escorted Lucifer through the outer courts, the inner court, past the attendants and into the Throne-room. He positioned Lucifer directly before the Throne with his commanders and lieutenants arranged behind him.

Stepping to his left, Michael joined his generals, captains and commanders, where they stood guard with the soldiers that had brought in more than eleven thousand of Lucifer's officers.

Gabriel and the officers of the Second Estate were on the other side standing guard, their swords drawn and glowing with the fire of Divine power.

Three trumpets sounded near the entrance of the Throne-room. Michael stepped forward and stood to the left and slightly in front of Lucifer.

Michael spoke in a loud voice that filled the Throne-room and echoed throughout the inner court, which was crowded with angels. "Your Majesty, Creator of all things, Judge of all things, at Your command we have assembled the rebels of the Third Estate in the area beyond the plain.

"We have brought the commanders and lieutenants of the rebellion before Your Throne. Lucifer, their leader, is here with them to be judged.

"Those who fled from the Third Estate to escape from Lucifer have been assigned places in the First and Second estates. There are others we felt should be judged separately because they did not actively participate in the rebellion. We will present them to You for judgment later."

Michael stepped back to his position with his officers. He drew his sword, as did all of his officers. Their swords began to glow with that same Divine power.

The three trumpets sounded again. Michael bowed down to the floor, facing toward the Throne. All of his officers bowed down behind him. On the other side, Gabriel bowed down also and so did his officers. The angels in the inner court bowed down as well. Some of Lucifer's officers also bowed down before the Throne.

Lucifer, standing in the center directly in front of the Throne, refused to bow. He looked about at his officers who were bowing and shouted, "Stand up, you fools, stand up. How dare you bow to anyone but me? I shall never bow to anyone again. Never! Do you hear me? Never, never, never will I bow down again."

Silence fell over the thousands of angels there in the Throne-room and in the inner court. All eyes looked toward the Throne and every ear listened intently.

The brilliant, unapproachable light from the Throne blazed and pulsated, then dimmed to the point where one could almost see the Throne. A voice that sounded like it came from eternity past and would roll into eternity future issued forth. It was tinged with sadness, yet authoritative and powerful.

"Lucifer My son, what have you done?"

Silence.

"Lucifer, I pleaded with you to not rebel. I gave you

opportunity to stop your mad quest for power. If you had only asked, I would have given you more. However, you didn't just want more power, you wanted what you cannot have, what you can never have.

"My love for you caused Me to exalt you and give you many things. But you despised the riches, the luxury and the authority I gave you. You wanted to exalt yourself even more and be like Me. You wanted to rule as I rule.

"There can only be one God, Lucifer. You cannot be God. Your rebellion has destroyed you. You have led twelve billion angels into rebellion with you. They must share your fate."

The voice of God paused for a moment. A feeling of grief and sad resignation swept over the Throne-room and spread to the inner court. The light emanating from the Throne dimmed even more and a cloud formed, enveloping the entire area of the Throne. A gloom settled over the whole room and the inner court, filling everyone with a sense of dread.

As God spoke again, it was obvious that His wrath was not eager, but came forth only as a last resort. His voice was filled with pity. It was as if He could hardly bring Himself to pronounce eternal judgment upon His beloved Lucifer and the angels of the Third Estate.

"Lucifer," He said, "you must be banished forever. To impress you with the enormity of your sin, I shall create a lake of fire---fire that burns with My eternal wrath. You shall be cast into that lake of fire and you shall remain there in burning torment forever and ever. All those who chose to join with you in your rebellion shall be cast into that lake of fire also."

Those words fell like boulders upon the ears of all who heard them. Shock waves rolled like thunder throughout the Throne-room and the inner court.

Lucifer's voice suddenly exploded, roaring vehemently, "You cannot do that to me! I will never submit to Your angry vengeance."

Turning to his thousands of officers, Lucifer shouted, "Attack! Attack! Don't let Him do this to me. We will leave this place. We will create our own kingdom. I will be your god. Come on, come on. Attack! Attack!"

Erhardnom, one of Lucifer's commanders standing nearby, said, "Lucifer, can't you see that we are unarmed? Can't you see that we are bound and helpless? Let's face it Lucifer, we are doomed."

Lucifer turned and faced the Throne again. "No! No! No!" he shouted. "You cannot do this to me. You have no right. You created me. You knew what I would do before You created me. You cannot punish me for doing what You created me to do.

"If I rebelled, it is Your fault," he continued. "You gave me free will. You gave me the power of choice. Now, You plan to punish me for using that power to choose. You are not fair. You are wrong."

Standing rigid and pointing the forefinger of his left hand directly at the Throne, Lucifer sneered in scornful contempt. "How can You call Yourself a loving God?" he growled, "and cast one-third of Your angels into a lake of fire? What kind of a God are You, anyway, that would do such a thing?"

God's answer was filled with compassion, yet firmly committed to righteous judgment. "Lucifer, I created you in My image. I chose to love you and to shower riches and honor and glory upon you. I wanted you to choose to love Me and obey Me. I did nothing to arouse resentment in you. I did not plant the seeds of pride in your heart.

"Never once did I harm you or hurt you in any way, yet you have chosen to break My loving heart and force Me to judge you. All creation is witness to the fact that some of your angels chose to reject your evil plot and escape your tyranny. They saw that worshiping you would be wrong.

"They used their free will to choose Me and My love. I shall reward them for their decision. Lucifer, I do not want to punish you, but you have left Me no alternative. I simply must reward you according to your choice."

Lucifer curled his lip, folded his arms defiantly and turned his back toward the Throne.

God continued His pronouncement of judgment. "Lucifer, you and those with you will not be immediately cast into the lake of fire. There are things that must be made very clear to you and all of creation about My love and My justice.

"First, you will be disembodied. You will remain without bodies for a time. Then, you will be given new bodies that cannot be destroyed by fire. You will finally be cast into the lake of fire, to suffer eternal torment, with no possibility of relief.

"Also, I will prepare a small planet in one of the presently expanding universes. There I will create beings much like yourself, except of a somewhat lower order. I will give them the same free will and free choice I gave you. They will not have the many advantages you have. I will even permit you to tempt them to disobey Me.

"If they choose to obey you, then you will rule over them. They will be your subjects. Their land will become your kingdom. Death will overtake them. I shall judge them and they will share your fate in the lake of fire.

"However, if they resist you and cry out to Me for help, I will help them. I will give them new bodies also and they will dwell in My presence forever. Then, all creation will know that My judgments are righteous and good. All created beings everywhere will understand that I am merciful and kind.

"From the beginning, when I created you, I set before you choices. I urged you to choose the good and avoid the evil. You made your choices in the full knowledge that what you were doing was wrong.

"That planet I will call 'earth.' The beings on it I will call 'humans.' You may go there and tempt them within the limits I shall prescribe for you."

Lucifer turned halfway around and sarcastically inquired, "And just where am I supposed to find this 'small planet' in a presently expanding universe?"

God answered with a sarcasm that startled everyone. "Why, Lucifer, you are so wise and knowledgeable that I am sure you will have no trouble finding it."

Michael and Gabriel were summoned and instructed, "Have the soldiers take the prisoners back to the holding area. Send all of your officers with them. You two stay here. I have further instructions for you."

Chapter Nine

Destruction

Michael and Gabriel dismissed their officers to accompany the troops that were taking the prisoners back to the holding area.

Persimal was assigned to escort Lucifer and was instructed to deliver him to Hasemadphen, General of the Second Division in the First Estate.

Surprisingly, Lucifer and all of his officers offered no resistance and began moving quietly out of the Throne-room, through the inner court, the outer court and across the plain.

Michael and Gabriel remained and presented themselves before the Throne, bowing low.

The light issuing from the Throne became brighter. As the Almighty Judge spoke, His voice was still somewhat sad, but marked with determination to do what is right.

"Michael," he said, "order your soldiers to disembody all of those who are condemned. Take their spirits to the gates of heaven and cast them out.

"Inform Lucifer that he will be permitted to come and see Me if he properly presents his request at the gates. I may at times order him to come here so that I may delineate the limits of his activities or reprimand him for attempting forbidden things.

"Gabriel, I want you and your angels to assist Michael in executing the prisoners and also in gathering up the carcasses of the slain. Take them to the Third Estate and dump them there.

"When you have done that," He continued, "I want you to completely destroy the Third Estate with fire. There must not remain a trace of it to be seen. My wrath will issue forth from your swords to burn buildings, stone, even the ground.

"All must be totally destroyed. The very residue of sin must be purged from our midst with fire. Give your angels specific orders to destroy the Third Estate so completely that one could not perceive that it had ever been there."

God instructed Gabriel, "Tell the attendants that after each time Lucifer returns here, they are to cleanse the very ground upon which he walks."

Then, speaking to Michael, God said, "Increase the guards at the gates. Any suspicious activity must be immediately reported to you and appropriate action taken.

"Michael, Gabriel, take the court attendants and other official workers, along with the entire First and Second estates, with you. All heaven must see the punishment of sinful rebellion. What they see will serve as a warning to reject selfish pride and not let it take root in their hearts."

The angels in the inner court, along with the Throne-room attendants, followed Gabriel and Michael to the outer court. There, messengers were sent to gather the other official workers throughout heaven. They accompanied them to the holding area.

Meanwhile, the prisoners arrived at the holding area and were divided into groups like the others had been earlier.

Lucifer, who had been quiet during the journey, spoke to Persimal. "Please let me ask a favor. This chain is giving me a great deal of discomfort. You can see how it burned my clothing and even my flesh. Please remove it from me. You can shackle me like the others if you wish, but please give me some relief from this awful burning chain."

Persimal obtained some shackles and draped them over his arm while he loosened the fiery chain.

Suddenly, Lucifer leaped upon Persimal, grabbing his sword and whirling around. "Now," he snarled, "I'm free and I'm armed. I am leaving here and no one can stop me."

Up into the air he flew and like a bullet streaked off in the direction of the Third Estate.

Elmer, one of the guards in Commander Ridni's district, saw what was happening and flew off in hot pursuit. Gerom, a commander standing nearby, took a dozen of his soldiers and rushed away to help Elmer.

Several guards who saw the commotion prayed, "Oh, God, please protect those who are going after Lucifer. Strengthen them to overcome him and bring him back."

Lucifer was faster than his pursuers. He flew directly to his palace and went inside, hoping to hide.

Elmer and the others arrived and surrounded the house. Gerom shouted, "You might as well come out peacefully. We have you surrounded and you cannot escape."

Lucifer did not answer. All was quiet. Elmer said to Gerom, "Shall we go in and get him?"

Gerom prayed, "Lord, what shall we do?"

The Spirit of God spoke in his heart, "Go, I am with you. I will strengthen you. You shall not fail."

Gerom walked around the house, giving careful instructions to each soldier. "Have your swords ready. When I signal, we will all enter the house through doors and windows. Remain quiet once we are inside.

"Whoever finds Lucifer must give a loud yell so the rest of us can come immediately to help capture him. Don't anybody try to be a hero. He is powerful and we must work together to overcome him."

Gerom returned to the front of the house and shouted,

"Charge!" Fourteen angels burst through the doors and windows and quickly looked around. Lucifer was not seen by anyone.

Slowly and cautiously they moved through the house, looking high and low, behind every drape and every piece of furniture.

Milnaper had searched three rooms and was now entering the library. He looked quickly about and then began a thorough search, keeping watch toward the door and the windows.

Behind the chairs, behind the drapes, under the study desk he looked. He was about to depart and go to another room when he noticed a ladder, used to climb up to the top shelves of books.

Milnaper then looked behind another chair or two, turned and walked out the door and closed it firmly with a loud click. He stepped away from the door and then softly and quietly stepped back and grasped the doorknob.

Flinging the door open, he looked high to the top of the bookshelves. There was Lucifer, peering over the edge.

Milnaper loudly yelled, "Library!"

Lucifer leaped through the air, sword raised to attack.

Milnaper turned to his right and ran as fast as he could down the great hall. Lucifer looked the other direction to see if anyone was coming and started after him.

Just as Lucifer passed the door of the butler's office, Gerom stepped out of the office behind him and shouted, "Hold it right there, Lucifer."

As Lucifer whirled to meet him, the other twelve angels came running from everywhere. They surrounded Lucifer, their swords pointed at him in a circle.

Elmer swung his sword like a flash of lightning. It severed Lucifer's hand above the wrist. Lucifer's sword fell to the floor, his hand still holding it.

Peerbehn, one of Gerom's angels, went into the great banquet hall, flew up to the ceiling and cut the chain holding one of the massive chandeliers. It fell to the floor with a crash.

He removed the other end of the chain from the broken chandelier and began dragging it toward the door. Turning to his left, he saw the huge mirror in which Lucifer had admired himself.

Peerbehn stopped, looked at the mirror and said, "You instrument of pride, I curse you in the name of Him who sits upon the Throne." Instantly, the great mirror shattered into millions of tiny pieces and fell like dust to the floor.

Dragging the chain out into the hall, he said, "Here, we can bind him with this."

"Thanks," replied Gerom. "By the way, what was all that noise in there?"

"Oh, I am so clumsy I broke a few things," he answered.

"Sure you are," chuckled Gerom. "The finest tailor in all of heaven and you are clumsy. Oh, sure you are."

"Well," said Peerbehn, "you know us tailors. We have hidden strength. Sometimes we just have to express ourselves. You know how it is."

They bound up Lucifer and took him back to the holding area and presented him to Hasemadphen as Michael had requested. Persimal went with them, reported his dismal failure and accepted full responsibility for Lucifer's escape.

Hasemadphen thanked him for his confession and integrity for not trying to evade his error or blame someone else. He said, "Persimal, Bilhameran will soon be conducting some classes that deal with personal responsibility. Would you be willing to be a guest speaker in them to share this incident and what you have learned?"

Persimal thought for a moment and then replied, "It will be embarrassing for me. In fact, I am downright humiliated by what I did. However, maybe a bad example is a good illustration. I'll do it."

General Hasemadphen looked at Lucifer for a moment and then spoke to Gerom, Elmer and those who had brought him. "He must have given you some trouble. I see you have made him left-handed. Please stay here and guard him a while longer."

Just then, Michael, Gabriel and the other angels arrived. They called the generals together and told them what God had ordered to be done with the prisoners.

After a brief conversation with Gerom, General Hasemadphen called Elmer forward. "Since you went immediately in pursuit of Lucifer," he said, "and then submitted yourself to Gerom and let him take command, you will have the honor of making the first strike of judgment for the justice of God and for all of us. You will disembody Lucifer."

Elmer raised his sword high. He looked at Lucifer and said, "You enemy of all righteousness, you father of all lies, you tempter of our souls, the judgment of Almighty God is upon you." He swung his sword downward, cutting Lucifer in half. The two halves of Lucifer's body fell outward. His spirit rose from the two and joined itself together in midair.

Michael and Gabriel raised their swords high and commanded, "Execute the prisoners now."

The angels of the First and Second estates quickly disembodied the rebels of the Third Estate.

All those who had not followed Lucifer to battle were kept aside so God could judge them separately.

Angels of the First and Second estates were divided into detail groups and given their assignments. About half of them were chosen to transport the slaughtered bodies back to the Third Estate and dump them there.

The other half were ordered to take the disembodied spirits of the Third Estate to the gates of heaven and cast them out. Lucifer was informed of his re-entry privileges and was warned to not try any activities outside of those specifically permitted by God Himself.

Additional guards were posted at the gates and the troops returned to the holding area to cleanse it. They were organized to march rank upon rank from north to south, waving their swords from side to side. The power beams burned the residue as they proceeded. Then, they marched from east to west doing the same thing. It was called, "grid cleansing." The stains of sin were completely eradicated.

All of heaven's angels then assembled some distance from the borders of the Third Estate. A line of troops surrounding the entire estate was placed near the border.

Michael and Gabriel pointed their swords toward Lucifer's palace and shouted, "Destroy in the name of God, the Supreme Judge of all creation."

Fire of the wrath of God beamed forth from their swords and Lucifer's mansion exploded in a blaze of divine fury. The other angels at the border pointed their swords out over the Third Estate. Flames of God's wrath flashed destruction upon everything in sight.

For what seemed about three earth hours, the fire raged. When all was completely destroyed, the fire stopped. The angels looked on in horrified wonder.

Palmoral spoke to Ezmarden and said, "Using our free will is a God-given right, but we must never use it to rebel against Him who created us. From now on, when I don't understand something, I will ask questions, but I will have my mind made up ahead of time to accept the answers and submit my will to the will of God our Father."

Ezmardan commented, "Yeah, me too. We have plenty of freedom to do what we want. We just need to stay within the guidelines given us. I think I am going to sign up for one of those classes on knowing and understanding the will of God. Do you know where one is being taught?"

"No," replied Palmoral, "but I am sure we can find out at the Central Academics Registrar's Office. I think I would like to sign up too. Let's go together."

Michael and Gabriel rose high in the air above the hosts of heaven to give instructions.

Gabriel spoke loudly, his voice booming like thunder over the twenty-four billion angels assembled there. "We are to go to our homes for a short period of rest. We shall then be called to observe a time of official mourning for our lost brothers.

"After another brief time of rest and refreshing, we will be invited to participate in a season of celebration and rejoicing for the cleansing of heaven and the expelling of iniquity and pride."

Michael dismissed the multitude with a command to rest and perform only the most necessary tasks.

They departed to their homes, traveling in groups, discussing the demise of the Third Estate.

Chapter Ten

Mourning And Celebration

After a season of rest, messengers were sent throughout the First and Second estates, calling them to participate in a period of mourning for the lost angels of the Third Estate.

The district commanders encouraged mourning for individual angels with whom they were personally acquainted.

After that, captains of sections organized large gatherings where many names of the fallen angels were read. Great lamenting was heard concerning some of the notable leaders of the Third Estate.

Generals over the twenty-four divisions called for massive demonstrations of grief for the loss of one-third of heaven's angels. Mournful songs were sung. Poems of sad reflection were composed and read in the huge gatherings.

General Hasemadphen composed a poem that would eventually become a song of sad remembrance to be sung at certain occasions of historical review. He read it to the angels in his division.

> Lucifer, Lucifer, how you have fallen.
> Your glory lies trampled in the dust.
> Your beauty deceived you till pride
> Overtook you and gave birth to lust.
>
> Lucifer, Lucifer, bright star of the heavens,
> So honored, so exalted by God's loving hand,
> You sought to exalt yourself higher and higher,
> And to do so by your own proud hand.

Lucifer, Lucifer, how you have fallen,
So far from your once lovely place,
To pain and eternal flaming torment,
To shame and the most awful disgrace.

Lucifer, Lucifer, father of all that is wrong,
We are warned to not follow your hate,
But to follow and imitate God's love,
Lest we also should share in your fate.

Lucifer, Lucifer, how you have fallen;
What tragedy, what harm and what loss.
Our hearts melt, our eyes weep bitter tears.
The price of sin is too terrible a cost.

Michael and Gabriel instructed the generals to prepare an enormous parade of twenty-four billion angels to walk past the outer court. They were to express their grief to God and their sympathy to Him for the awful judgment He was forced to pronounce upon Lucifer and the Third Estate.

They were divided into large groups, each group pouring out its feelings with wailing, songs, poems, banners, instruments and other displays of sorrow.

Sufficient space between the groups was maintained so their sounds would not overlap. At the front of each group, twelve huge trumpets sounded. They were so large that two angels were needed to carry each trumpet while a third sounded the mournful tones.

One by one, the groups stopped in front of the outer court, conveying messages to God the Father. Some groups shared their sympathy with the heart of God for the pain He was suffering. One expression was from the Third Division of the First Estate. It read like this:

O Lord, You created them. You provided for them. You loved them and desired their love in return. But they turned away from You. They broke Your loving heart. Your commandments they hated. Your love they despised.

The time for judgment came and You grieved. Your heart was torn inside Your breast. Love for Your creation cried out for mercy. Mercy was then extended. Your mercy pleaded with them to repent and change.

Mercy was rejected and pride ruled supreme in the hearts of the rebels. They cried out for freedom. They desired to be free from the God who created them. They chose Lucifer to be their god. They believed his lies.

Your justice, Your righteousness, could not allow Your mercy to turn away from doing what is right. Your wisdom could not allow their pride to continue. To do so would have sown the seeds of corruption everywhere.

O Lord, You did not want to destroy them, but for our sake and for Your holiness and righteousness You banished them. You consigned them to the fire forever. Our tears mingle with Yours. What anguish and loss.

The time of mourning lasted the equivalent of forty earth days. On the fortieth day, God left the Throne-room, walked through the inner court and out to the far edge of the outer court.

There He stood, surrounded by clouds, bright light flashing forth. He spoke in a voice that could be heard by all of the assembled angels. "Our season of mourning is over. We shall not forget our precious fallen ones. Our hearts hold fond memories of long ago when our fellowship with them was sweet and beautiful. Lovely thoughts of them linger like perfume in our minds.

"However, we must also remember their evil deeds, their rebellion. Your hearts must be firmly committed to doing what is right. Please do not ever let the seeds of pride take root in your hearts and begin to grow. Pride goes before a fall.

"Go to your homes now and rest. Do only the most necessary work. After you have rested, we will celebrate our victory over sin and rebellion."

The angels went to their homes exhausted. They refreshed themselves with baths, light meals and trips to the River of Life where they swam and enjoyed its life giving flow. About seven earth days were needed to complete the rest and refreshing.

When trumpets were sounded to begin the celebration, the commanders told their angels to visit in small groups and cheer each other with songs and stories of God's protection of them on the battlefield.

The captains planned banquets, great feasts, throughout the First and Second estates.

Generals organized huge parades in each of their divisions. The music was loud and joyous. The songs were exuberant.

Michael and Gabriel planned a massive gathering to praise God and celebrate the cleansing of heaven. The angels of the First and Second estates were mixed, joining together in high praise to God, blending their hearts and voices to exalt Him who rules upon heaven's Throne.

The generals were given opportunity to speak concerning their divisions. The captains and commanders under each general carried banners and paraded before the Throne to express joy and thanksgiving to God.

Gabriel gave a great speech. Here are a few brief excerpts from it: "Let praises unending be poured out before Him who sits upon the Throne of heaven. He is worthy of all the praises our hearts can feel or our minds conceive. He has done great things. Let all creation bless His holy name...

"Michael gave himself to praising God and obeying His commandments. His generals saw his devotion to God and imitated it. Happy is he who hears the command and obeys it. Joyful ecstasy is the result of cheerful obedience. As the generals taught all those under their command, joy spread throughout the entire First Estate...

"I, Gabriel, who often stand before the Throne of Him who creates all things, have learned to trust Him who created me. I do not always fully understand His commands, but I know they are good and will result in joy when I obey them. I have never regretted doing His will...

"My generals also saw my joy and communicated it to those of lower rank. The Second Estate has long been bathed in joy...

"A great while ago, Lucifer began to disagree with God. He felt he deserved more respect and honor. The seeds of pride rose up in his heart and grew. They produced bitter fruit, the fruit of rebellion. That fruit eventually poisoned most of the Third Estate. They lost all their joy…

"When that rebellion became known to us in the First and Second estates, we began to be very concerned. We began to lose our joy…

"God, our Father, the Judge of all creation, saw our sad and worried faces. He judged the evil ones. He cleansed our abode of the sin that killed our joy. We now celebrate the great victory He has given us over depression and sin. We did not gain this victory by ourselves. Our God has given us the victory…

"Some time ago, in super-universe number seven, a large planet of created beings challenged the Creator. I was sent to warn them of the direction their plans were taking them. They listened and repented. God rewarded them for casting down their plans and submitting to His wisdom…"

When Gabriel finished the speech he led the hosts of heaven in singing a song of praise and thanksgiving to God.

After that, Michael gave a speech. A few words from his speech are also worthy of note: "My friends, we are truly blessed. Our God, our Creator, has absolute power over us. He created us and He could destroy us if He chose to do so. However, He is not angry and vengeful; He is merciful and kind. We all have made mistakes, but He does not condemn us for mistakes. It is rebellion that He must judge…

"Our celebration is as much a celebration of God's mercy and love as it is of the victory He has given to us in battle…

"What horrors would befall us if God's nature was like that which Lucifer chose for himself…

"Oh, to be more like my God who created me is my constant prayer. The deep desire of my heart is to grow more and more into His image. He is my Father and He has created something of Himself in me. My heart grieves when I disappoint Him…

"Some time ago, one of my commanders made a proposal that I thought was worthy of God's personal attention. When I stood in His presence and spoke of it, the cloud parted, the bright flashing light receded and I saw His face. He smiled and said, 'That's a good idea. Go ahead and do it. And if you think it appropriate, give that commander a promotion'…

"Our God seeks only our good, never our harm. That is why it is always right to obey Him. Sometimes when you don't understand His will in a particular matter, remember that He also has a very good sense of humor. I have resolved several questions in my own mind by remembering that…

"As we bring our celebration to a close, we can go to our homes and jobs with our joy renewed and with love and appreciation for God in our hearts…"

Michael finished his speech and was about to dismiss the crowd when the ground began to shake. Twenty-four billion angels bowed low, facing toward the Throne-room.

God came to the outer court as He had done before and spoke to the assembled multitude.

It is interesting to note that while others often use a great many words to express themselves, God frequently communicates His thoughts to us more succinctly.

He said, "You have soothed My heart with your kind words and joyous music. I particularly enjoyed one of your banners which read, 'We decided to stay COOL.'"

A roar of laughter and applause rose from the crowd. When it subsided, God continued, "I also lost My joy over the tragic events we have recently endured. Now, My joy has returned.

"I give you My blessing. I give you My joy. Go in peace."

The great throng began to disperse. Some of the angels flew quickly home because of work that needed to be done immediately. Others walked along leisurely, discussing various matters.

Ridbaral and Egalitmor were discussing the fate of the angels found hiding in the Third Estate. "Do you know if they have been judged yet?" asked Egalitmor.

"I don't know," replied Ridbaral. "I suppose they are still in custody somewhere. I wonder if they will be condemned like the others?"

"Well," said Egalitmor, "they did hide from Lucifer and refuse to fight for him. That should count for something."

"That's different," reasoned Ridbaral. "They didn't escape and ask for help like the others did. They just hid like cowards."

They walked along in silence for a moment, then Egalitmor spoke. "Those angels had to choose between obeying Lucifer their archangel and their own personal commitment to the Creator. Sometimes our leaders are so close and God seems so far away that we get confused."

"You're right," replied Ridbaral, "You know, if God does spare them and if they are integrated into our midst, I think they should be encouraged to develop their personal relationship with the Spirit of God that dwells in them."

"Yes," said Egalitmor, "we do not often see and hear God up close like we did today, but we can always be guided by His Spirit. I don't know how He does it, but He sits on the Throne and at the same time occupies all of creation. He lives in our hearts and is always willing to guide us if we just take time to listen to His Spirit speaking to us."

"Oh, look," said Ridbaral, "I see Midherpen and Gulapigol. Let's go visit them a while. I have some things I need to see them about, anyway."

Ridbaral and Egalitmor turned off the road and greeted their friends.

....

Things quickly got back to normal. The refugees from the Third Estate were absorbed into the First and Second estates and given jobs befitting their talents.

Marlann brought Thomlin to Gabriel and presented him for judgment. Gabriel said that God himself must judge matters as serious as this.

Michael, Gabriel, General Hasemadphen, Ehmlar and Marlann escorted Thomlin and the twenty-four thousand nine hundred and fifty-two angels found hiding in the Third Estate to the outer court and waited for permission to bring them into the Throne-room for judgment.

When the trumpets sounded, the prisoners were taken into the Throne-room and arranged in long rows. They all bowed down with their faces to the floor and waited.

The voice of God spoke from the Throne and said, "Please, everyone, stand up." They rose and stood silently.

Michael gave a brief statement of why they were there. God spoke and said, "Bring Thomlin forward." Marlann escorted him forward and stood beside him.

The voice of the Almighty Judge spoke in gentle tones. "Thomlin, you simply followed orders until your conscience forced you to decide. You chose to beg for mercy. You did not rebel against Me. Go with Marlann. He will provide for you."

God's voice rose in volume. "The rest of you were

102

timid and fearful, but you risked the wrath of Lucifer in order to avoid fighting against Me. You did not escape, as did the others, but you did hide from him and come peacefully when you were found.

"I want half of you to go with Michael and half with Gabriel. You will be given new jobs, new homes and a new start with leaders who will love you and guide you into My perfect will."

They all bowed down again, tears of joyful relief flowing from their eyes.

Thomlin went with Marlann. Michael and Gabriel divided the rest of them and departed, thanking God for His mercy and kindness.

Joy again filled both estates with songs and music.

Chapter Eleven

Good Plans, Evil Plans

God invited Michael and Gabriel, the twenty-four generals and the two hundred and eighty-eight captains into the Throne-room to share with them the next step in His dealing with the doomed Third Estate.

They gathered by rank, bowing to honor Him who sits upon the Throne.

Although God knew beforehand the outcome of this meeting, He invited heaven's officials to participate in order to increase their understanding of His judgments.

This was a very important meeting. These top officers were soon to learn more about God than they had ever known before. His nature would be revealed to them in a way that would change their understanding of Him forever. Justice and mercy, holiness and forgiveness, judgment and redemption would be reconciled.

How could God be holy and still be merciful? How could He be just and still forgive those who sin? These questions were about to loom large in the minds of those who were bowing before Him.

"Please rise," echoed His voice from the Throne. As they stood to their feet, they witnessed something that neither angels nor man can fully comprehend.

The cloud receded and the light dimmed. In the center of the Throne sat the majestic figure we know as the Father.

To His right sat one who would wear many titles. Among them, The Word, The Lamb, The Redeemer. To His left sat another figure, the one called the Holy Spirit.

How He can be One and yet express Himself in Three has been debated for centuries. Perhaps eternity will answer our questions. The Scriptures assure us that we shall someday see Him face to face and that we shall know as we are known.

The central figure on the Throne began speaking. "You were here when I told Lucifer that I would prepare a place called 'earth' and create beings on it called 'humans.'

"Although I will give them the power to choose good and reject evil, under the subtle temptations of Lucifer and his angels, those humans will choose evil.

"I do not wish to destroy them, but My justice demands that they be punished just like Lucifer and his followers. Let Me ask you this question. How can I rescue them from the judgment of fire after they have sinned and followed Lucifer into disobedience?"

The archangels, the generals and the captains stared at each other. A few of them whispered in quiet tones. No one could think of a reasonable answer.

Bergundi, a captain under General Hasemadphen, spoke up. "Your Majesty, couldn't they just repent and change like we do when we make a mistake?"

"Rebellion is not a mistake," replied the Father. "Fredmorgan made a mistake, suffered the consequences and is now recovering. Those who chose to obey Lucifer are guilty of rebellion. They must be punished. I want to be merciful, but I must be just. How can I rescue those humans from the judgment of their sins?"

Bergundi replied, "Lord, when Lucifer and his angels rebelled, they did so in full knowledge and in haughty pride. You told Lucifer that You would permit him to tempt the humans. If he deceives them and tricks them into disobeying You, isn't that unfair?"

"No, it is not unfair," answered God. "But it is precisely because of that disadvantage that I want to rescue them from the punishment My justice demands. I want them to choose whom they will serve. If they choose Lucifer they will share his fate. If they choose Me after they have sinned, how can I rescue them?"

Bergundi thought for a moment and then spoke. "Lord God, Creator of all things, this conversation is beyond my ability to continue. I really have no idea how they can be saved once they have sinned against Your holiness and righteousness. However, I choose to trust that if there is a way, You will find it."

The Father looked down from the Throne upon all of the high officials of heaven and said, "Bergundi is trusting Me to do what is right, even though he does not fully understand. My heart earnestly desires that every angel in heaven will trust Me the way he does.

"Now, the problem we have is that those humans will disobey Me and we must find a way to redeem them. Sin must be punished and the only way to remove their sin from them is to find someone who is totally innocent and blameless to put their sin on.

"Someone here in heaven must go to earth and live a perfectly sinless life and die for them. That someone must bear all of their sins in his own body. That innocent person must be sacrificed for them. He must die in their place. His blood must be shed to atone for their sins.

"One more thing, that person must become a human and be subject to Lucifer's temptations just like them."

There was silence for several moments. The angels were in deep thought. Quiet whispers began in small groups. Then, one angel stepped out and stood directly in front of the Throne. It was Tubilar, a captain under General

Pergalite in Division One of the First Estate.

"I will volunteer to go," he said. "However, I have a question. What will become of me when I give my life for them?"

The Father replied, "Tubilar, I appreciate your willingness to help those whom you do not know, who have not yet even been created. You have a problem, though. You are not perfect. Your sacrifice could not satisfy My perfect justice and holiness. Not only that, I know you better than you know yourself. If I were to send you there, Lucifer would defeat you. You would sin and need redemption yourself. However, thank you for being willing to try."

Gabriel and Michael went aside for several moments and quietly discussed the matter. The other angels watched, but could not hear what was being said. They saw heads shaking, hands gesturing, shoulders shrugging and weight shifting from foot to foot.

Finally, the two archangels turned and walked back to the center, in front of the Throne.

Michael spoke, "Your Majesty, we don't know of anyone who is worthy to be the perfect sacrifice that Your holiness demands. We do, however, like Bergundi, believe that if there is a way to redeem the human sinners, You will find it.

"Furthermore, our long and intimate association with You leads us to believe that if there is no way, You will make a way. This problem is too great for us. You are the Creator. You have perfect understanding. You possess all wisdom and knowledge."

Gabriel added, "We also know that Your great heart of love will not create beings and then just destroy them. From the day You created us, You have shown us divine love. Never once have You harmed us. No, You would not create them if You could not redeem them."

Gabriel turned and looked at the more than three hundred angels. They were nodding their heads in agreement.

Turning again to face the Throne, he said, "I think I speak the thoughts of all of us here. Your judgments are just. Your motives are pure. Our hope is in You, Lord. Our life is in You.

"You created us in love. You have sustained us in love and You rule us in love. You will never, ever, do anything wrong. While we cannot answer Your question about how to forgive sinners, we rest assured that whatever You do will be right."

God the Father looked to His right at the One who is called 'The Word' and then to His left at the One called 'The Holy Spirit.' His eyes then surveyed the angels. When He spoke, the sound of His voice was kind and gentle.

He was about to reveal Himself and His nature to them in a greater way, but He didn't want to embarrass any of them because of the words they had spoken or the offers they had made. He also did not want to appear haughty or overbearing. God wanted to reveal His love and His plans in such a way as to draw His angels closer to Him.

"My thanks to all of you," He said, "for your suggestions and your concern for those humans that we know will fall into sin." The Father paused for a moment and then said, "We are still left with a great question. Who can I send? Who is able to go and do this for us?"

The angels stood silent. Then, Michael and Gabriel dropped to their knees. All the other angels bowed down on their knees also. Every eye was fixed upon the Throne.

Suddenly, The Word rose from the Throne, stepped down, knelt at the feet of the Father and said, "I will go. Send Me."

A gasp swept over the Throne-room. Shock electrified the angels kneeling there. They didn't speak. They just looked at each other, dumbfounded.

Every mind silently asked the same question, "How can this be? Can God sacrifice Himself to Himself for those creatures that don't even exist yet?"

The Father turned to the Holy Spirit and said, "This is the only way it can be done." He then turned to the One kneeling before Him and said, "You will be called 'The Lamb slain from the beginning of the world.' You will bear the sins of My people. You will redeem them."

He turned again to the Holy Spirit and said, "We must begin right away to prepare the planet so it will be habitable for them. They will be created from the dust of the ground, but they shall be in our image and likeness. However, they must be of a little lower order than the angels."

The cloud gathered again about the Throne. The light flashed brighter and brighter until the angels could not look at it. The One who would be known as The Lamb rose and stepped up into the light and the cloud.

The Father's voice came forth. "Thank you all for coming. Go to your homes and your work. Many of you will be given assignments on earth. You will assist Me in the great work of redemption."

....

Meanwhile, Lucifer and his angels set up camp some distance away from heaven's gates. They organized meetings throughout the huge camp to discuss what they would do. Three more generals were appointed and began attending top level meetings with Lucifer.

At the first big meeting with the generals, Lucifer outlined some beginning procedures. "First of all," he said, "we shall change our names. I shall choose several names and titles for myself: Satan, The Adversary, Dragon, Serpent and others that I will invent from time to time.

"I shall retain my name, Lucifer, the Light Bearer, only to deceive those who walk in darkness. Darkness! Darkness! Yes, that's it! I will call my kingdom the Kingdom of Darkness.

"I renounce the image of God in which I was created. I will be the very opposite of Him who so arrogantly judged me. I refuse to look like Him. I refuse to be like Him. I refuse to talk like Him, except to deceive those creatures on the planet He calls 'earth.'

"I am sure He will make that planet beautiful. I want you to corrupt it and make it ugly. He will probably create those humans in His image. I want you to change them into our image. Most likely, He will plant beautiful gardens with sweet aromas and perfumes. We will change that planet into a stinking garbage dump.

"I believe He will try to dwell inside their bodies and fellowship with their spirits. I want you to deceive them into rejecting His Spirit and welcoming you to possess them in body, soul and spirit.

"That planet will become my kingdom. Those humans will become my slaves and I will force the Almighty Judge to damn every one of them to eternal fire.

"I have other things to say to you, but I will do that later. Right now, I want you to remember this---When we have defeated His purpose on earth and proven Him wrong, I shall march triumphantly up to His Throne and demand that

He set us free.

"He is so just and righteous that He will be compelled to damn His precious humans to the fire He is preparing for us. He will be forced to let us go free.

"I must have your absolute loyalty. You must obey me in everything. Don't forget, our eternal destiny depends on our defeating Him. We must not fail."

Chapter Twelve

And God Created

Satan posted lookouts to watch for anyone who might depart from heaven because that would be the surest way to find the planet earth and the humans God would create.

Sure enough, it happened. A great procession of angels accompanied the Holy Spirit to heaven's main gate. He began His journey slowly, almost as if He didn't know He was being watched.

Satan took Baalmeg, Elgitlar and Pubilentre, his three newest generals and followed. Gradually, the Holy Spirit picked up speed, while the four evil spirits maintained a distance of about eight thousand earth miles. Somehow, they really believed the Holy Spirit did not know He was being followed. Oh, how deceived are those who are self-deceived.

The Holy Spirit finally reached a speed that is beyond our ability to measure. Twenty-three super-universes were passed before He began to slow down. "Aha!" said Satan, "It looks like He is headed for super-universe twenty-four."

Gradually decelerating, the Holy Spirit passed by more than a billion universes in super-universe number twenty-four. Selecting a universe toward the near edge, He slowed down even more. A galaxy that would later be called "Milky Way" was chosen. Then, a small star that we know as "Sun" was approached.

Finally, a tiny planet orbiting that sun was selected. The planet was in utter chaos. The Spirit of God circled and observed. It was covered with water. The Holy Spirit began to move like a mighty wind over the waters.

Some time was spent preparing the planet for human habitation. Pressure from the hot center of the globe forced dry land to push up out of the waters. Enormous evaporation caused billions of tons of water to rise and be suspended in the air.

Depressions left by the rising land areas became the resting places of the remaining water. These are called "seas" or "oceans." Vast underground caverns formed by the boiling heat from the center of the earth were filled with water to cool the surface of the ground to a temperature suitable for vegetation and animals.

The steam thus generated carried more water high into the air. In such a greenhouse environment, plant life flourished. When the waters were properly evaporated, the sun and moon and stars appeared and divided the rotation of the earth into days and nights.

Great whales and sea monsters swam in the now pleasant oceans. Fish of every kind filled the seas and inland streams. Animals roamed the earth, feeding upon the lush grasses and fruits. Birds flew above and swooped down to feed on seeds and grass.

God was pleased with the newly prepared planet. He walked around, enjoying the results of His labor. It would be a marvelous home for the humans about to be created.

Satan and his three generals were watching everything that God was doing. They watched Him plant a beautiful garden in a place called "Eden."

They watched in bewildered amazement as God took some dust of the ground and formed it into something that resembled an angel. He then breathed into it the breath of life and that dust of the earth became a living creature.

Satan whispered to his generals, "He has breathed a little

of Himself into that hunk of dirt, that human being. It looks somewhat like an angel. It looks something like Him. We must find a way to destroy it. We must not allow Him to succeed with His little experiment."

The man that God had created was far superior to all of the animals He had called forth from the earth and the sea. This human being, however, could not do many of the things angels do. He was earthbound. He was somewhat less than an angel.

"This is going to be easy," said Satan. "You just watch me. I will cause him to sin and rebel against God."

Satan waited until God was some distance away from the man. Walking toward the man, Satan plotted in his mind how he might deceive him.

Suddenly, a mighty angel appeared out of nowhere, blazing with divine light and wielding a shining sword. Satan stopped in his tracks, stunned by the sight of him.

"You cannot approach the man yet," said the angel. "You must wait."

Satan snarled, "Hey! I have authority from the Almighty Himself to tempt this man. Get out of my way."

"You must wait," replied the angel.

"Well," demanded Satan, "just how long must I wait?"

The angel answered simply, "You must wait."

Satan scowled and walked away, muttering curses and blasphemies as he went. He had a meeting with his generals to discuss what to do. They decided that for the time being they would just watch closely everything that was happening.

God was somewhere in the garden, while the man He had created was walking about, exploring the area outside.

Satan and his generals were lurking nearby, observing the man and wondering what would happen next.

As God came out of the garden and walked toward the man, Satan said, "Look! He doesn't look like He did yesterday. He looks more like the One called 'The Word.' He looks more human. Perhaps that is so He can better communicate with the man. I suppose next He will appear as the Father. Maybe I should go up to the Throne and find out what is going on here. This thing is getting more complicated every day."

God invited the man to come and see the garden. Satan and his generals followed at a discreet distance, about an eighth of a mile.

The garden was very large, about two miles long and two miles wide. The man would be quite busy cultivating it even though there were no thorns, no weeds, no destructive insects or disease to harm the garden.

It did not have the paved walks, the carefully constructed flower beds and vegetable gardens that Satan remembered in the Third Estate. Rather, it was a beautiful mixture of trees scattered here and there, with vines and bushes bearing many kinds of fruits and berries.

Some of the trees and bushes bore nuts. Herbs and spices gave fragrant aromas to the air. Vegetables grew in patches not shaded by trees.

A river flowed through the garden, providing water for all living things there. Animals in the garden were vegetarian, as was the man at that early time in history.

Outside the garden, huge beasts roamed the earth, foraging in the forests and plains. Others waded in the rivers and lakes, feasting on the lush grasses and plants.

Birds built their nests in trees and rocky crags, while fish swam in the delightfully pure waters.

The tremendous underground reserves of water, warmed by the hot core of the earth, caused a mist to rise up from the ground and water the face of the earth.

Lucifer and his generals sneaked closer and hid in some bushes, watching and listening as God talked with the man whom He had created.

"This garden will be your home," God said. "You may explore outside the garden, but you will find it much more comfortable here. There is plenty of food here for you to eat and plenty of work for you to do.

"I am putting you in charge of this garden to tend it and keep it beautiful. Also, you will have dominion over all the animals. The first thing I want you to do is give names to the animals.

"Your name is Adam, or Ruddy, because I formed you from the dust of the ground and the color of your skin is somewhat like the color of the dust from which you came.

"So, use the mind that I have given you. As you observe the animals, think up some good names for them."

It would take a long time to name all of earth's creatures. So, while God was nearby, listening, Adam named only a few that first day. There were large cattle, small animals, birds, giant beasts and insects to be named.

"Hmmm, you are so beautiful," said Adam, "with your black and orange stripes. I think I will call you 'tiger.' And you there, with the spots, you will be called 'leopard.' Oh, my! What a large creature you are. I will call you 'elephant.'"

Just then, an enormous animal came walking by. It was about a hundred feet long from head to tail and weighed many thousands of pounds. Adam studied that awesome creature for a moment and then said, "I think I will call you 'dinosaur.'"

Turning to God, he said, "I feel hungry. Are the fruits of all these trees good for food?"

"Well," replied God, "I'm glad you asked. You may eat the fruit of every tree---except one."

"And which tree is that?" inquired Adam.

God spoke clearly and forcefully, "There is a tree in the midst of the garden. See, it is right over there, that one. You must not eat the fruit of that tree. It is the Tree of the Knowledge of Good and Evil. The day you eat of that tree you will surely die."

"What does 'die' mean?" Adam asked.

"Trust Me," answered God. "You don't want to know. Just do not eat the fruit of that tree."

"All right," said Adam. "If You say so, I won't."

It was dusk and God left the man alone in the garden. As day faded into night, Adam found a soft patch of grass and laid down to sleep.

God began making daily visits to the garden to talk with the man, instructing him and answering his questions.

A beautiful fellowship developed as they walked through the garden and discussed the events of the day. Adam would share his discoveries and tell of the many names he had given to the animals, trees, bushes and fruits.

Meanwhile, Satan and his generals were busy discussing how they might get the man to eat of the forbidden fruit.

Baalmeg suggested, "Maybe we could cause some of that fruit to fall at his feet when he walks past the tree. Surely he will pick it up. Perhaps he will eat it."

"Not a real great idea," replied Satan, "but it's worth a try. You go and see if you can get him to eat it."

During the next several weeks they tried more than a dozen schemes to trick the man into eating the forbidden fruit. All attempts failed.

The guardian angel that had been assigned to protect Adam was difficult to get past. Only some of the less forceful plans were permitted to be used by Satan and his generals. It was very frustrating, but they kept inventing new and different ways to tempt the man.

One day, God came to visit the man in the morning instead of the evening. Adam was sitting on a rock, watching the animals play and graze and rest. "Greetings," God said. "How are things going today?"

"I have been watching the animals," Adam replied. "I see that there are two of each and they are male and female. They help each other and they enjoy playing together. However, I am all alone. I have no one like me, no one to help me cultivate and tend all of the fruits and vegetables.

"I really enjoy Your daily visits and our wonderful fellowship together, but I would like to have a person, a human like me, a female to be with me, just like You have provided for all the animals. When You are not here in the garden with me, I sometimes get very lonely."

"Very well," replied God, "I shall make a companion for you. I shall do it differently from the way I made the animals, though. I shall take a bone from your side and form it into a woman, a female, for you."

God caused a deep drowsiness to come over the man. Adam began to yawn and was soon fast asleep. God opened the man's side and removed one of his ribs. He then closed up the flesh and carried the bone about six paces away from the sleeping man.

Elgitlar was watching. He ran to Satan and the others, excitedly bidding them to come and see what was happening. They rushed into the garden, hiding behind nearby trees, peeking out to observe the creation of the first woman.

God took the bone, gently blew His breath on it, stroked it with His hands and spoke words to it that Satan and the others could not quite hear.

The bone began to grow. Larger and larger it grew. Flesh appeared, blood formed, skin covered it over. Hair grew out of the scalp and fell gracefully to the shoulders of the now completed body.

The woman opened her eyes and breathed her first breath. She looked into the eyes of her Creator and said, "Hello." Then, she turned and looked over at the man lying on the ground and felt an instant kinship with him.

God brought her close to the man, left her standing there and He disappeared.

Adam slowly awoke, feeling pain in his side. He looked down and saw a great wound there. That scar would remain and continually remind him of the wonderful thing God had done for him. He carefully rose to his feet.

He turned around and standing there before him was a creature that looked something like himself. As he gazed in wonder, he could see that this was a female counterpart of himself, just like the male and female of the animals.

There was a difference, though. This creature was taken from his body, not from the dust of the ground.

She spoke, "Hello." Her voice sounded different from his. It was a beautiful sound. He reached out and touched her skin. It felt somewhat different than his.

The woman was actually created from a part of his body, but she was not exactly like him. The difference was exciting. Something in him awakened. She was the perfect complement to him. She was the perfect companion.

She spoke again. "God created me to be here with you." The sound of her voice was like sweet music to his ears.

"Wow!" he said. "This creature is actually bone of my bones. She is flesh of my flesh. I will call her 'woman' because she was taken out of man."

The voice of God spoke from above. "Adam, she was not taken from your foot that you might have dominion over her as you do the animals. Neither did she come from your head so as to rule over you. I took her from your side so that you may love her and hold her always close to your heart. She is a living part of you."

Adam looked up toward heaven and said, "Thank You, God. You have given me a perfect companion. I shall never be lonely again."

Turning to the woman, he said, "Come, let's take a walk. I will show you the garden. It is our home. God provided it for us. Everything we need is here: food, water, things to see, things to do. We shall be busy.

"I am really glad you are here to help me," he said. "I will show you the kinds of work we will be doing. God has explained many things to me. I will share with you all that He told me."

Adam continued, "There is a great big world outside the garden. Perhaps tomorrow we will go out and explore some of it. However, this garden is our home and provides all that we will ever need."

Walking along hand in hand, they began getting acquainted and enjoying the fresh air, the sights and sounds and smells of the beautiful garden there in Eden.

Chapter Thirteen

One Little Bite

Adam was showing the newly created woman the trees, flowers, animals, fruits, nuts and berries that he had named. "There," he said, "that bush there. See the berries on it? They are black, so I call them 'blackberries.' And this tree here, the fruit on it I call 'plums.' Would you like to taste one? I think you'll like it."

"Yes," she replied, as he pulled one from the tree. The woman tasted it and exclaimed, "It is delicious."

The couple continued on their way, unaware they were being watched. Satan, Baalmeg, Elgitlar and Pubilentre were following along behind them, close enough to hear some of what the man and woman were saying.

Pubilentre whispered, "All of our attempts to get the man to disobey God and eat the forbidden fruit have failed. Let's watch the woman carefully. Maybe we can trick her into eating it."

"Whatever we do," said Satan, "we must do it soon. We don't want to give her time to learn how to resist our plans. We must sneak up on her and catch her when she is the most vulnerable."

"That's right," agreed Baalmeg. "We must approach her when the man is not with her. We must find her alone when there is no one to help her."

"Yeah!" said Elgitlar. "Have you noticed that she does not yet have a guardian angel like the one protecting the man? We'd better get to her before one is assigned."

Satan started to speak but was interrupted by Pubilentre.

"Look!" he almost shouted. "They have stopped at the forbidden tree. Let's get closer and listen to what they are saying. Maybe we can find a way to deceive them."

"I'm hungry," exclaimed the woman. "Let's eat some of this fruit," she said, reaching her hand upward.

"No!" shouted Adam, grasping her bodily and pulling her away from the tree. "That is forbidden," he said firmly. "God told me that if I ever eat of that tree I will surely die."

"What does 'die' mean?" asked the woman.

Adam replied, "I don't know, but the way God warned me about it I think it would not be good. Whatever 'die' means, I don't believe we want to do it."

"Are you sure I will die if I eat it?" inquired the woman. "I mean, I am different from you. Maybe I won't die."

"You were taken from my body," he replied. "You are bone of my bones and flesh of my flesh. However, when God comes to visit us this evening I shall ask Him to explain more about it.

"Come on," he urged. "Let's find another tree. Oh, here is a good one over here. You will like its fruit. I call it 'orange' because of its pretty orange color."

Satan and the others knew they must hurry. They must watch for their earliest opportunity to tempt the woman. They followed the couple for about half a mile.

Adam stopped and sat down. "I'm a little tired," he said. "I think I'll take a nap." Lying down on the soft grass, the man was soon asleep.

The woman did not feel at all tired. She was alert and curious. She wanted to continue exploring the beautiful garden on this, her first day of life.

Walking among the trees and bushes, she stopped now and then to examine fruits and nuts. She noticed that most of the fruit was soft, while the nuts had hard outer shells.

A green bush bearing blackberries caught her attention. She picked one of the berries and tasted it. Finding it to be delicious, she picked several more and ate them.

Looking up, she saw the forbidden tree. Something aroused her curiosity. She felt drawn to that tree. She moved closer and closer, wondering why it was forbidden.

A voice came from the midst of the tree. "Hello," it said. "Are you enjoying your walk?"

"Oh, yes," she answered. "Everything is so lovely. My name is Woman. Has Adam given you a name yet?"

"My name is Serpent," was the reply.

The woman said, "Come out so I can see you."

Down out of the tree came the serpent and moved over to her left. The woman had no way of knowing who Satan is or that he had entered into the body of a serpent to tempt her. She had no reason to be suspicious.

"Why are you called 'Serpent,'" she asked.

"I am the most subtle of all the creatures God has made," he replied.

"And what does 'subtle' mean?" she inquired.

"Oh, you'll find out soon enough," the serpent answered. "Right now, I want to ask you a question. Did God say that you must not eat any of the fruit of the trees in this garden?"

"No, He didn't say that," responded the woman. "He said we may eat the fruit of all the trees except one."

"Which one is that?" queried the serpent.

She replied, "This one right here. He said we must not eat of it or even touch it or we will die."

"What does 'die' mean?" asked the serpent.

"I don't know," answered the woman, "but Adam said it probably would not be good to die."

The serpent said, "Listen to me. You will not die. Let

me tell you why God doesn't want you to eat the fruit of this tree. He knows that when you eat it your eyes will be opened and you will become like Him. You will be wise and you will know both good and evil."

"What is 'evil?'" questioned the woman.

"Well," responded the serpent, "It's kind of hard to explain. You will have to eat it and find out for yourself. It just works that way."

The woman looked at the fruit. "It certainly is beautiful," she remarked.

"Yes, and so tasty, so delicious," prompted the serpent.

"Will it really make me wise like God?" she asked.

"Of course it will," assured the serpent.

The woman reached up and picked a ripe, plump piece of fruit. Holding it in her hand, she wondered what 'wise' meant. It sounded good. She wanted to be 'wise.'

Seeing her hesitate, the serpent said, "Come on, taste it, just one little bite."

She raised it to her lips, sunk her teeth into it and bit off a portion. Chewing it slowly, savoring the flavor, she enjoyed it immensely.

A thrill of discovery flowed through her, tingling her senses. She had done something by herself without Adam being there to tell her she mustn't do it.

"I think Adam will be proud of you," said the serpent. "Why don't you give him some of the fruit so he can be wise too?"

"That's a good idea," she responded. "I think I'll do that right now."

She turned to go, holding the partly eaten fruit in her hand. Then, turning back, she said to the serpent, "I don't feel any different and my eyes don't see things differently."

The serpent reassured her, "It just takes a little time.

You'll see. Hurry on, now, and give some to your husband. I'm sure he will be very pleased with you."

She walked briskly back to where the man lay, still sleeping. "Adam," she called as she approached. "Adam, wake up. I have something for you."

The man opened his eyes and sat up, stretching and yawning. "What is it?" he asked.

"Look what I found," she said. "It is delicious. Here have some."

He looked at the half eaten fruit and then into the eyes of his wife. "Isn't that the forbidden fruit?" he asked.

She replied, "I ate some of it and I didn't die. See? Here, taste it. It'll make you wise."

Adam looked at the fruit and again at his wife. She didn't look any different. "Well," he said, "maybe just one little bite. But no more. Do you understand? Just this once."

"Yes, if you say so," she agreed. "Just this once and never again. I won't even go near that tree any more if you don't want me to. Here, just take one little bite."

She leaned close to him and raised the fruit to his lips. He hesitated for just a moment, then bit off a piece and began chewing it. "Mmmm, it does taste good," he said. "Let me have some more."

They devoured the fruit and agreed that it was indeed delicious. Adam said, "I don't feel any different, do you?"

"No, not yet," replied his wife, "but the serpent said it might take a while for us to notice a difference."

"The serpent?" inquired Adam.

"Yes," his wife responded. "The serpent said it might take a while for us to become wise. He also was very confident that we would not die. He said the reason God didn't want us to eat that fruit was because we would become like God, knowing good and evil."

Adam said, "I didn't know that serpent could talk. He never talked to me. Let's go over there and discuss this with him some more. Maybe he can give me some answers that God hasn't given me. Come on, let's go."

They started walking in the direction of the Tree of the Knowledge of Good and Evil. As they walked, they saw several animals and Adam told his wife the names he had given them.

Suddenly, he stopped. She stopped and turned around and inquired, "What's the matter?"

He looked at the animals and then at his wife. "You know, these animals have fur coats. You and I have nothing to cover our skin. We are naked."

A feeling of great embarrassment swept over the woman. "Oh, my goodness!" she exclaimed.

Adam said, "It is almost dusk. God will be coming to visit us any minute now. We can't let Him see us like this."

The woman asked, "What shall we do?"

"Well, let me think," her husband replied. "We've got to find something with which to cover ourselves. Look, the leaves on this fig tree. Let's see if we can fasten some of them together and cover our nakedness.

"Hurry! Help me! Don't just stand there. Get moving. We don't have much time."

They managed to sew enough leaves together to cover part of their bodies. They still felt awfully uneasy about God coming and finding them like that. The fig leaves seemed terribly inadequate. They needed more than fig leaves to cover their embarrassment before God.

"What if He asks us about the forbidden fruit?" said the woman. "Will He be angry? Oooooh," she wailed, "I wish I had never eaten that fruit. I don't feel good. I don't feel wise. I feel awful. I feel downright stupid. Oh, why, why did I listen to that serpent? Why? Why? Why?"

"I told you not to eat that fruit," shouted the man. "I told you what God said and you went ahead and did it anyway. Now, look what a mess you've made of things. If I die, it's your fault. Do you hear me? It's all your fault."

She looked up into his face, her eyes blazing, and said, "Hey, Mister, don't you talk to me like that. You ate it too. You are just as guilty as I am. And another thing, I was created just today. I don't know any better. And you, you've been around for a while."

The woman continued, "You shouldn't have gone to sleep and let me wander off by myself like that. No sir, it's not my fault---it's your fault. If this is any indication of how you are going to take care of me, I am in big trouble. I sure won't be able to depend on you for my safety."

They hadn't noticed that the serpent was nearby, relishing every moment of the confrontation, savoring every unkind word they flung at each other. His generals watched with great interest the whole scene.

"Well, boys," hissed Satan from the serpent's mouth, "I did it; I really did it. I got them both to sin. I got them to disobey God. We're on our way, guys. We're on our way to victory."

Satan boasted, "When he obeyed me and ate that fruit, he gave up his dominion over the earth. He doesn't know it yet, but he gave me the title deed to the whole planet. It is my kingdom now. I shall rule with an iron hand. That man and his wife will become my slaves."

The four of them stood there, watching Adam and his wife blaming each other. Satan and his generals congratulated each other again and again.

Just then, the woman heard a sound. "What was that?" she gasped.

"It's Him," replied her husband. "Quick, let's hide over here in these bushes."

"Do you think He will find us?" she cried.

Adam answered, "I don't know. I just don't know."

They quickly ran into the bushes and waited.

Chapter Fourteen

Now What Do We Do?

God was walking along, enjoying the beautiful garden He had created. It was the cool of the evening, about the time He came each day to visit. Sometimes He would find the man in one part of the garden and sometimes in another.

The man had always run joyfully to meet God and excitedly tell Him of things he had discovered. Then, he would ask questions and listen intently while God answered and explained.

This time, however, the man did not come running and the newly created woman was nowhere in sight.

Satan, still dressed as a serpent, was near the forbidden tree, confident that God would soon be there. He had been rehearsing what he would say to God on this fateful day.

"I shall say to Him," he muttered, "Aha! Your little experiment didn't work, did it? Look at them. They sinned. They disobeyed You. You have failed. They are mine, my slaves. The earth is mine. It is my kingdom.

"Oh, yeah!" boasted Satan, "I shall look right into His face and tell Him He is a failure.

"I shall say to Him, You are unfair. You cannot possibly throw me into the fire now. If you do, You will have to throw them in with me. I guess I outsmarted You this time, didn't I?"

Just then, God came walking through the trees, His feet softly treading on the lush green grass. His clothing was bright and shining, His eyes glancing this way and that.

He always appeared a little different than the previous

day, displaying some new facet of His nature and personality. This day He seemed especially kind and cheerful. There was a glad spring in His step as He walked along and He was singing a happy little song.

> Bumblebee, bumblebee, how do you fly?
> But fly you do, bumblebee. My, O My!
> Your body's so big and your wings so small,
> It's really a wonder you can fly at all.

> I made you, bumblebee; I made you that way,
> So man in his quest for knowledge someday,
> Will look at your wings and body and say,
> "How did God do that? How wondrous His ways."

Now, God already knew what would transpire and how the man and woman would respond, but He wanted to give them as much opportunity as possible to admit their sin and ask forgiveness.

As God approached the forbidden tree, Satan felt a sudden sense of foreboding. He couldn't understand why, because God seemed so cheerful.

The three generals dashed into the bushes and hid, peeking out and wondering why they were so afraid.

God called out in pleasant tones, "Adam. Adam. Where are you?"

Silence.

"Adam, where are you? Please come here," God called.

Slowly and cautiously, the man crept out of the bushes and stood, embarrassed, on one foot and then the other. His head was tilted downward and his eyes looked this way and that upon the ground. His hands were twisting together in front of him, brushing against the fig leaves that covered a portion of his body.

"Why were you hiding?" God asked.

The man responded, "Well…I…uh…when I…uh… heard the sound of You walking in the garden…uh…I… uh…I was afraid…so I hid myself in the bushes."

"You've never been afraid of Me before," said God. "Why were you afraid this time?"

Adam slowly answered, "Because…uh…because I didn't want You to see me naked. That's…that's why I was afraid."

God paused for just a moment and then softly said, "Adam, look at Me."

He waited for the man to respond.

Silence. Awful silence. Adam did not look up.

Satan was beginning to recall the hateful words he had rehearsed to hurl at God. He could almost envision God killing the man right there beneath the forbidden tree.

The Serpent hissed quietly to himself, "I have destroyed His plan. I have won my case. I have defeated Him. I am the god of this world."

Adam still did not look up into the face of his Creator. He twisted and turned in embarrassed shame and disgrace.

The daily visits had always been such a delight. Now, he just wished God would go away and quit looking at him.

Finally, God spoke and questioned, "Adam, who told you that you were naked?"

"Well," answered the man, "nobody told me. I just noticed it today and I didn't want You to see me that way. I was embarrassed."

God asked, "Is that why you draped those fig leaves around your body?"

"Yes," replied the man.

The tone of God's voice was both instructive and loving, as when a father gives guidance to an erring child.

"Adam," He said, "it will take a great deal more than fig leaves to cover you and your sin against Me. Have you eaten some fruit from the forbidden tree?"

The man felt such pressure to justify himself that he simply could not admit his disobedience and accept responsibility for his actions.

The Serpent was hissing in diabolical satisfaction as he watched the difficult exchange between the man and his Creator.

Finally, Adam looked up and glared insolently into the face of God. "It's not my fault," he said through clenched teeth. "It's that woman YOU gave to be with me."

Adam turned and shouted into the bushes, "Woman, come out here. Come out here right now."

There was no response.

The man strode violently into the bushes and dragged the woman out, flinging her to the ground at God's feet.

"It's her fault," Adam growled, rage coloring his face and hot tears forming in his eyes. "She picked fruit from that tree. She gave it to me and I did eat."

God did not lash out in fierce angry tones, speaking revenge upon Adam. He did not want the man to view God as an angry, vindictive ruler, harshly punishing those who fail to completely obey strict and arbitrary laws. He wanted the man to understand that it was his sin, his disobedience, that brought consequences.

Looking down at the woman cowering on the ground, God spoke gently, "Please stand up."

She stood, her head turned to one side and her eyes downcast. She felt all alone, abandoned and forsaken. The man who was to be her protector and provider had turned against her, blaming her for his own sin. God, who had created her, was standing there looking at her and asking questions she did not want to hear or answer.

"Please look at Me," said God in soft and gentle tones.

The woman turned her head slightly and lifted her eyes upward just enough to see the face of her Creator. Her face felt hot. Her body shook with a trembling she could not understand. She only knew she could not bear to have God stand there, looking at her like that.

God spoke, "Tell Me what you've done and why you did it."

She looked at Adam. He was standing there with his arms folded across his chest, glowering at her. She glanced again at God. His eyes looked into hers, waiting for an answer.

Anger, fear, resentment and humiliation all swirled around inside her. Blood rushed to her head and face. Her eyes felt such pressure that everything seemed to appear slightly red in color. She decided she was not going to take the blame and cover up for those who were as guilty as herself.

Pointing at the serpent, she pursed her lips, wrinkled her brow and said, "It's his fault. He's the guilty one---him, that serpent right there. He tricked me. He lied to me. He deceived me and that's why I ate the fruit."

God looked at the serpent. He knew Satan was inside that snake, but the man and the woman did not yet know about Satan, the fallen angel.

First, God spoke to the reptile in order to dramatize a lesson and a warning to all future generations that sin lurks in hidden places, ready to strike us when we stray from the pathway of righteousness.

He said, "Because you have done this terrible thing, you, more than all other animals in the world, are cursed. You will crawl on your belly and eat dust all the days of your life. From this day on, you and the woman will be deadly enemies. Your children and hers will hate each other."

Then, God said something to the serpent that was more than a curse upon an animal. His voice had an ominous tone in it that spoke far more than tragedy for snakes that slither on the ground. Satan knew that God was speaking directly to him.

God's voice thundered judgment, "You will strike the heel of her Child, but He will crush your head."

Those words would perplex and haunt Satan for thousands of years. He certainly did not know the full meaning of what he had just heard from his Creator.

Turning to the woman, God said in less ominous tones, "In great pain you shall bear children. However, you will always long for your husband to be kind and loving and affectionate to you, even though he will rule over you and sometimes mistreat you."

Adam was listening to the curses upon the serpent and the woman. He was beginning to think maybe he would escape punishment. Suddenly, God fixed His gaze on the man. His face became more serious and His voice much stronger. His eyes pierced to the depths of Adam's soul. It was an awful moment.

God said, "Because you have listened to your wife's pleading and have yielded your will to hers, because you have eaten the fruit that I absolutely forbade you to eat, I will curse the ground on which you stand.

"Throughout all of your life," God continued, "the ground will resist your efforts to till it. Thorns and thistles and weeds will attack your fields. Birds, animals and insects will devour your crops.

"You will spend your years in hard labor, struggling to cultivate food for your family. Your descendants will pause to wipe the sweat from their brows and curse you for the legacy of toil you have given them."

God concluded His pronouncement of judgment by saying, "The ground will not easily give you food. You will labor long and hard to obtain it. You will sweat and toil until the day you die. I formed you from the dust of the ground and you will surely return to the ground from whence you came."

The man and woman stood there shocked and dismayed, but resentful, not willing to admit their guilt or to ask forgiveness of their sin.

Satan left the body of the serpent and joined his generals in the bushes. They cursed God, cursed the man and woman, cursed the serpent and everything else in sight. They cursed until they could invent no more vulgarities and blasphemies. Rage and hatred consumed them. They wearied themselves spewing evil words.

After a long silence, God spoke tenderly to Adam and his wife. "Come with Me," He said, "I want to give you something."

The pair followed Him quietly, glancing at each other now and then, wondering what was going to happen.

God led them to a place near the entrance to the Garden of Eden. He turned and said to the man, "Call two animals to come here."

Adam looked around for a moment and saw two beautiful rams grazing nearby. "Come here," he called, motioning with his hand. They came at once, nuzzling him and looking up at him with gentle, trusting eyes.

One of them rubbed playfully against him, dislodging the apron of fig leaves. Adam pushed the animal away, picked up the apron and held it in front of himself.

God struck the animals, killing them right before the

eyes of the man and his wife. He then stripped off the skins, leaving their bloody carcasses lying there. Adam and his wife were sickened at the sight.

God fastened the skins around the bodies of the two horrified people and said, "See, I have made clothing to cover your shame. Look at what I have done. It cost these two animals their lives to provide clothing for you. Their blood was shed for you."

Then, God looked up into the air and began speaking as if He were talking to someone they could not see. They listened as He spoke, "Now the man is like Us and can understand the difference between good and evil. We cannot allow him to stay here. He might pick fruit from the Tree of Life and eat and live forever."

Turning toward the garden entrance, God looked back, motioning with His left hand and said, "Come with Me."

The man and woman followed Him out of the garden toward the West. About a hundred feet away, near a large rock, God stopped and turned around. The distressed couple turned around also and looked back. What they saw terrified them.

Several mighty angels had appeared and were standing guard. A large sword, blazing like fire, was there, turning in every direction.

God said, "You may never again enter the Garden of Eden. If you try, they will kill you. It would be best for you to go some distance away from here."

Adam and his wife looked for a moment at the angels and the flaming sword. There was no way they could get back into the garden. They were homeless.

Turning again, they were shocked to see that God had disappeared. They were alone, abandoned, frightened. The woman grasped her husband's arm, looked helplessly up into his eyes and asked, "Now, what do we do?"

Chapter Fifteen

Lord, Where Are You?

Adam and his wife walked westward for a short distance, then turned and walked south several miles. They wondered how they would survive outside their garden home. Could they find enough food? Would the animals outside the garden be friendly or hostile?

It was dark when they stopped to rest in a pleasant plain. In those early days of human history, the Persian Gulf extended farther north and west than it does now. The couple made their first campsite about two miles west of the gulf, not far from a small stream.

A chill wind blew across the plain. The skins they were wearing smelled so bad they discussed whether to just take them off or try to leave them on. Adam said, "Maybe we could turn the wool side to our bodies. The wet side feels terrible against our dry skin."

They removed them and turned them inside out, but soon discovered the wool was scratchy and made them itch. It was not a pleasant night. Adam and his wife huddled together under a tree. They didn't sleep much.

That new environment was not nearly so comforting as the garden. A feeling of dread foreboding surrounded them.

The animals moaned and screeched and howled in fear and confusion. Something was different that night. Sin had entered their world. Those humans were out of harmony with creation. The terrible disharmony frightened the animals.

When the sun rose the next morning, the man and his

wife began looking for something to eat. They found a bush with some berries on it. It was a meager breakfast, but it would have to do. Later, they found some wild onions and ate them. It was not long until they had a stomachache. Drinking lots of cool water helped a little.

Discovering several fruit and nut trees, as well as wild vegetables and berries within walking distance, they decided to stay there instead of wandering too far away.

A shelter of leaves and branches was constructed to protect them from the heavy dew that formed each night. A bed of soft grass made sleeping more comfortable.

However, weeds were springing up out of the ground and thorns were appearing on some of the bushes. Thistles were sprouting and growing with amazing speed. The search for food became increasingly difficult. Injured hands and feet were a daily problem.

One morning before they began their quest for breakfast, Adam was rubbing his bruised feet and thorn-pierced hands. He said, "You know, if we are going to stay here for a while, I think I will give this place a name."

"I have a name for it," said his wife, "Briarpatch."

"No," replied Adam, "I'm going to call it 'Eridu.'"

"And what does 'Eridu' mean?" inquired the woman.

Adam looked at his feet and hands, then at the scratches and bruises on his wife and answered, "It means 'My awakening to sorrow' because every morning when we wake up I feel sorrowful."

"Yeah, me too," she said. Examining her feet, she continued, "Look at my feet, how cut and bruised they are. Is there any way we can protect our feet from the thorns and sharp rocks?"

Adam thought for a moment and then suggested, "Maybe we could kill some animals and wrap their skins around our feet."

That sounded like a good idea to the woman, so they went out before breakfast, looking for animals to kill.

Some of the smaller animals were so fast they ran away and could not be caught. Some of the larger animals fought back and presented mortal danger to the couple.

After about an hour of trying and failing, they decided to find some food and discuss hunting strategies.

Adam thought maybe they could get a sharp stick and poke an animal with it. His wife suggested that she might walk around and scare an animal toward Adam, who could then throw rocks at it.

Several attempts with a long sharp stick ended in failure. Throwing rocks was tried next. The woman frightened a young deer and as it bounded toward Adam, he took aim with a rock about the size of his fist and threw it with all his might.

The rock struck the deer in the face, stunning it momentarily. Adam quickly leaped on the animal and broke its neck. Obtaining a larger rock, he crushed its skull.

"Help me get the skin off," he called to his wife. He pulled at the animal's skin with his hands. After a few moments of effort, they realized they could not skin the deer with their bare hands.

The woman found a sharp rock and cut the skin from the neck down over the belly. It took a while and a lot of hard work, but they managed to remove the skin and carry it back to their campsite.

Adam started to cut the skin into four pieces but his wife said, "Here, let me wash this thing first and then dry it before we cut it."

"Okay," was her husband's reply, "that sounds like a good idea. Maybe it will be easier to cut and won't itch."

They made wraparound boots for themselves, even learning how to cut thin strips of leather and tie them securely to their feet. Later, they cut and sewed them to fit their feet better.

The little shelter of leaves and branches was blown away in the wind, so they obtained more skins and made a tent of them. That served as a much better place to sleep.

One day, while they were exploring the area, they saw two lions attacking an ox. What a bloody mess. After the lions had killed the ox, they began eating it. Soon, other animals came to eat also. Birds hovered nearby, waiting for an opportunity to partake of the bloody feast.

Turning away in horror, Adam and his wife returned home, discussing the awful thing they had just witnessed.

"Adam," the woman inquired, "do you think those animals might eat us?"

"I don't know," he replied. "I sure hope not."

Looking at the small shelter made of skins, the woman said, "If those animals decide to eat us, this little tent won't give us much protection. Is there any way we can make a stronger one?"

Adam replied, "Maybe we could get some rocks and stack them up. That would keep the animals out."

She countered, "I haven't seen very many flat rocks around here. These rocks would very easily fall over on top of us."

"We could try to flatten them," he offered.

His wife inquired, "How would we flatten them?"

"I don't know," was his reply.

"Hey, I've got an idea," said the woman. "Do you remember that mud pit we saw the other day? Around the edges it was dry and hard. Maybe we could put mud between the rocks and when it dries it will hold the rocks together.

Adam closed one eye, twisted his mouth to one side, thought about it for a moment and then commented, "It's worth a try."

They spent several days building an igloo shaped dwelling. First, they bent large branches together, tying them at the top and fastening the bottoms to the ground. Then, they placed rocks and mud over that frame, leaving an opening at the front for an entrance.

When the mud dried, the new dwelling seemed solid enough. "Now," said the woman, "how do we keep the animals from coming through the entrance to attack us?"

Adam looked around and then said, "We could roll a big rock in front of the entrance."

"Bad idea," said the woman. "Now, what do you think of this?" she asked. "Suppose we extend the entrance out and make it small enough that we have to crawl in. Then, we can fix it so we can put a small log across the opening at night to keep the animals out. In the morning we can remove it and go in and out."

The entrance was successfully completed in one day. They felt safer at night after that.

Once their cooperative efforts to effect safety were completed, it was not appreciation, but resentment that arose between them. On several occasions the arguments became so violent that Adam struck his wife and knocked her to the ground.

He resented her ideas being better than his. He especially hated the way she found fault with his ideas and pushed so hard to bend him into doing what she wanted him to do.

Adam went farther and farther away to hunt, leaving his wife to tend the garden they had planted and make clothing for both of them.

She spent her days angrily doing chores and rehearsing terrible accusations that she would hurl at him when he returned.

One day, Adam started out to hunt and his wife called after him, "When are you coming back?"

"Maybe never," he replied. "Living with you is worse than living alone."

She stood there, watching as he walked away. Hot tears filled her eyes. "How could he be so cruel?" she cried bitterly.

Adam walked about a quarter of a mile, then turned around and looked at his wife standing there, her head in her hands, weeping.

"Why does it have to be this way?" he asked himself. "Why can't we be happy together? She is supposed to be a helper for me, but she is always telling me what to do. I don't think she likes me at all." He walked away, glad to escape the yelling.

After about a week of hunting, he had two large skins and several smaller ones. He was just starting toward home when a bear came out of a thicket and attacked him, mauling him severely. "Lord, where are You?" he cried. "Please help me."

Just then, one of the more aggressive dinosaurs came walking by. It saw the bear, smelled the blood and became enraged. A chemical reaction inside the dinosaur caused something that looked like smoke and fire to come out of his mouth and nostrils. He pawed the ground, snorted loudly and charged the bear.

The bear was no match for that monster and was soon torn to pieces by the huge clawed feet and the enormous teeth. The dinosaur lumbered off, roaring and belching fire and smoke.

Adam was badly wounded and bleeding, but he was alive. He realized that he had nearly been killed by the bear. Looking up toward the sky, he said, "Lord, I don't know if You sent that creature to rescue me, but if You did, thanks."

Meanwhile, the woman was experimenting with something she had found while exploring the area. The seeds from those flax plants yielded oil, but the stems were fibrous and could not be eaten.

As she sat near the house one day, twisting some of those fibers with her fingers, she suddenly got an idea. Maybe she could make thread from them and sew things together.

Another thought came to her. What if she could put many threads side by side and then fasten them together with others woven through them in the other direction. "Say! That would make much softer clothing than these skins," she said out loud.

Adam had been gone almost two weeks now, and she was beginning to accept the fact that he might never return to her. She wept several times daily over the terrible arguments they had and the bruises and cuts he had inflicted upon her.

The cuts were healing well and the bruises were fading. She wondered if she would ever see Adam again. Was he building a rock shelter for himself out there somewhere? Maybe wild animals had eaten him. Perhaps tomorrow she would go in search of him to see if he was alive or if she could find anything remaining of his body.

"If he comes back," she said softly to herself, "I'm going to try to not argue so fiercely with him. I don't want him to hit me. Oh, why can't he just come home and put his arms around me and hold me and tell me he loves me?

Why does he have to be so mean to me? He blames me for everything that goes wrong.

"Oh, dear God," she cried, "if You'll just send him back to me, I'll try to be more of a helper to him and less of a boss.

"I need him, Lord. I need him to do the heavy things I cannot do by myself. I need him to be with me and love me. I am so lonely that I almost don't want to live anymore. Please, God, please bring him back to me."

Adam had been limping along for several days. The bear had torn a large patch of skin from his right leg. His right arm was broken just above the wrist where the bear had bitten him. The bear's claws had ripped open the skin from his left shoulder down across his body to his right hip.

Infection had set in and pus was oozing from the wounds. Flies, gnats and other insects were tormenting him mercilessly. He trudged on, determined to get back home and see his wife once more before he died.

Stopping to rest near a small stream, he washed his wounds, hoping the insects would be less aggressive. He sat on a rock at the edge of the stream and wondered if he would be able to make it all the way home. He was still several miles away. If another animal was to attack him, he would not be able to defend himself.

He looked up toward the sky and said, "God, I don't know if You can hear me, but if You can, I need to talk to You. Are You listening? Can You hear me?

"You gave me a wonderful woman to be with me and help me. I have been awfully mean to her. I've blamed her for all my mistakes. I've blamed her for my sins.

"Am I really to blame for all this? Is it really all my fault? Why can't she just shut up once in a while and quit nagging me? I'm doing the best I know how. Why does she expect more of me than I am capable of doing? It seems like no matter how hard I try, she is never satisfied.

"Lord God, I'm in trouble. I may die before I get back to her. Please, God, don't let me die out here. I need her. I need her real bad. Oh, God help me get home. Please, please help me get home to her.

"I promise, Lord, I promise, if You help me, I will never be mean to her again. I will love her. I will tell her how much she means to me. I will appreciate her. I will do nice things for her. God, I don't know what to do for her. I don't know what she needs. Please tell me what to do."

The voice of God sounded like a deep echo, floating in on the gentle breeze. It surrounded Adam with its soft, yet majestic tones. God spoke to Adam as a wise father speaks to a distressed son.

"There are many things you need to learn about your wife and how to live happily and peacefully with her. However, for right now, I will give you two suggestions.

"First, pick some beautiful flowers to give to her.

"Then, apologize for the cuts and bruises and all the hateful words you said to her.

"Oh, yes, a third suggestion, treat her with courtesy and kindness, just the way you want her to treat you.

"I guarantee that you will like the results."

Chapter Sixteen

Homecoming

Somehow, the woman believed that God heard her prayer and that her husband would return to her. She decided to fix something to eat and pretend that he would be home just in time for supper.

She gathered some vegetables, put them into a little basket she had woven out of reeds and soaked them in a hot spring that was bubbling up out of the earth. She had found that the hot water softened the vegetables and even changed the taste of them somewhat.

If Adam should come home, she would be ready to greet him. Oh, how she wanted him to come back to her. She missed him so.

She had taken some large pods and fashioned bowls from them. They were nice dishes in which to put the hot vegetables. She had then sharpened some small sticks that could be used to spear the food and lift it to one's mouth.

Animal skins had been stretched over a wooden frame to make a small table for two. The pod dishes were there, the sharpened sticks beside them.

She turned and looked toward the Southwest, the direction her husband had gone two weeks before. Her eyes were blurred with tears and she could not see the crippled figure hobbling toward her. A silent prayer rose from her heart, "Please Lord, please."

Wiping the tears from her eyes, she looked again. What she saw shocked her. It was Adam. He was hurt. Her heart leaped and pounded with a whirl of emotions as she ran to meet him. "Adam, Adam," she cried. "What happened? What happened?"

Exhausted and in great pain, he crumpled to the ground. Adam weakly said, "A bear...a bear got me...tried to eat me. A dinosaur came and killed it...saved my life."

She put her arms around him, hugged him and kissed him and tearfully said, "I was so worried. I thought I'd never see you again. I'm so glad you're home. Please don't ever leave me again like that."

With her help, he slowly and painfully rose and walked to the campsite. She washed his wounds and applied some of the oil she had extracted. That soothed him somewhat and also discouraged the insects that had tormented him so.

She propped him against a large rock and moved the table over to him. "What is this?" he inquired.

"I've been quite busy while you were gone," she answered. "I made these things so we don't have to put our food on the ground. Look, I cooked these vegetables in the hot water of that spring over there. And these little sticks, see how you can use them instead of your fingers?"

Adam started to discount those inventions as unnecessary, when he remembered what God had told him earlier that day. He looked at his wife. Her eyes were wide and expectant, waiting to see if he approved. He began to realize that she had done these things for him. She really was trying to be the helper God had created her to be.

"This is nice," he said. "Oh, oh, my goodness!" he exclaimed. "I picked some pretty flowers for you out there, but I must have dropped them when I fell down. I'm sorry."

"That's all right," she assured him. "I was so concerned about you that I guess I didn't even see them. There will be lots of times you can give me flowers. I'll remind you."

They ate the meal happily, with Adam praising his wife

for the table, the dishes and the cooked vegetables.

After the meal was finished, the woman washed the dishes in the hot spring and put them back on the table to dry. She helped her husband walk the short distance to the nearby stream. They sat there, listening to the gentle sound of the flowing water.

Adam's broken arm felt better now that his wife had wrapped it tightly with some large leaves and tied them with leather thongs. She also poured more oil on the awful wound on his leg.

She looked up and prayed, "God, I asked you to bring my husband home to me and You did. You made his body and I believe You can heal these terrible wounds. Please, God, make him well."

Adam looked at his wife. Tears filled his eyes and ran down his cheeks and into his beard. He put his left arm around her and laid his broken right arm in her lap.

His voice cracked as he spoke. "Sweetheart, I know now what it feels like to be hurt really bad. Can you ever forgive me for the terrible things I did to you? I hit you with my fists and I hurt you bad, real bad. I'm sorry. I'm so sorry."

"Your words hurt me worse than your fists," she replied. "When you hit me, your fists hurt my body, but your words hurt my soul, my spirit. You can see that my body is healing up well, but my spirit is still broken. Oil and bandages can't heal a broken spirit."

Adam looked at the bruises and cuts on her face and tried to imagine the hurt she was feeling inside. He said, "I guess God used that bear to teach me something. I had no idea that my words could hurt you so much.

"I promise," he said, "I promise I will never hit you again. I'm sorry for all those hateful words I said to you.

"Oh, God, why have I hurt the woman You gave to be with me? Help me to understand her. Help me to love her. Help me to be the husband she needs."

His wife looked up into his eyes and said, "I need to be forgiven too. I said a lot of mean things to you. Tell me, does your spirit hurt when I yell hateful words at you?"

"Yes," he replied, "but not in the same way your spirit hurts. When you yell at me, I just get angry and want to start breaking things."

"I'm glad we are talking instead of yelling and hitting," she said, pressing her scarred face against his torn chest. "I have a suggestion," she offered. "When we feel like yelling and hitting, let's just remember that bear."

For the next few days they practiced being nice to each other and helping each other. When one of them would start to argue, the other would growl like a bear. They began to learn each other's likes and dislikes.

Patience promoted understanding and understanding promoted love and love promoted patience and patience...

In that pristine environment their wounds healed quickly. There were scars, but within a month they were well and feeling strong. The scars were silent reminders that selfishness and anger can bring serious and long-lasting consequences.

One day, Adam and his wife were sitting on a hillock, overlooking a beautiful meadow. The sun was warm, but a gentle breeze was wafting over the tall grass, bringing the sweet scent of wildflowers to the resting couple.

Animals were grazing nearby, keeping wary eyes on the humans who brought sin and disharmony into the world.

After a while, Adam said, "Look, do you see what those two animals are doing? Over there, that male and female. That is how they produce little ones."

"Do you suppose," inquired his wife, "that we could produce little humans if we did that?"

"I'm sure we could," replied Adam. Suddenly, a feeling rose within him that literally took control of him. That feeling blotted out all thoughts from his mind except one. The hillside and the meadow faded from view. His eyes looked at his wife and somehow she seemed different, beautiful, desirable. He felt as if he was going to explode.

He pushed her down and began kissing her face. "Please, not now, not here" she said, pushing him away. "Not here in front of the animals."

"Why not?" he asked, "They did it in front of us."

"Well," she replied, "I just don't feel right about it out here in the open, with them watching us. Maybe tonight, in our home, in our bed. Maybe you could pick some flowers for me and say nice things to me."

Adam couldn't see any reason to delay, since he was quite ready and eager, but he thought it might be best not to force her. Was this another one of the things about her that he must learn to understand? Would patience bring understanding? Would understanding bring love? Would love bring...?

"I'll tell you what," said his wife, "Let's go home and I will cook the best supper you ever had. And then, we can go walking in the moonlight. And then, we'll go home where we can be all alone, just you and me, with no animals watching us. And then..."

It happened just that way. Adam learned a lot about his wife that day. He did have some questions, though. Would he have to pick flowers every time? What if there was no moonlight?

Well, somehow she seemed nicer than before, more beautiful, more...something. They were now really joined together and Adam was truly happy. He would do everything in his power to please her and protect her and provide for her.

She drifted off to sleep in his arms and he breathed a silent prayer. "Dear God, thank You for creating her and giving her to me. Not only is she bone of my bones and flesh of my flesh, we are now truly joined together. We are truly one. Please, God, teach me how to love her so I may teach our little ones how to be happy."

Days stretched into weeks and weeks into months. One day, Adam said to his wife, "It seems like an awfully long time since the way of a woman has happened to you. Do you suppose you are going to bring forth some little ones?"

"Maybe," she replied. "I have felt different lately. Twice this week while you were out gathering fruit for our breakfast, I felt as if I couldn't eat a thing. As a matter of fact, I was gagging and spitting. However, by the time you came back with the food, I felt better and was able to eat."

More days and weeks passed. Adam noticed that his wife would cry for no apparent reason. She insisted that he search far and wide for food she had not wanted before. She even woke him up in the night sometimes to go and find food for her.

One day he said to her, "You've been eating too much food lately. Your tummy is getting awfully big."

"Come here," she said. "Put your hand right here."

"Hey!" he exclaimed. "Something is moving in there."

Her skin seemed softer, her eyes brighter. A beautiful smile formed on her mouth as she spoke. "A little one is forming inside me. When it comes out, I must devote my time and energy to caring for it and feeding it. You must stay close to home and help me."

Adam said something that would result in a lot of hard

work. He asked, "Where will we put it?"

"We will need a much larger house," she replied. "You had better get started building it right away."

He wished he had not asked the question, but he knew their little shelter of rocks, sticks and mud would not be adequate. They could only crawl into this one at night and sleep. To care for a baby, they would need a house big enough to stand up and walk in.

"I could get a lot of animal skins and make a big tent," he suggested.

"No!" was her emphatic reply. "That will not do. Wild animals can tear a tent down and eat us all. We must have a big strong house with a big strong door to protect us."

Adam thought about the mechanics of constructing a large stone tent and was not happy about the prospect of all those rocks, held together with mud, hanging up there over his head.

"We need flat rocks," he said, "but there are only a few around here and they are so big I cannot move them. If only we could find smaller flat rocks..."

"I have an idea," offered his wife. "The mud around the edges of that mud pit dries almost as hard as a rock. Maybe we could get some mud and shape it like flat rocks and when it is dry we could build our house with them."

Adam was beginning to really appreciate her ideas. It bothered his ego somewhat that he had not thought of it first, but he would take that idea, add his ability to work out the details and claim it as his own. He would be in charge. He would make the decisions.

The woman would soon learn how to feed ideas to her husband without arguing and trying to exert her will over his. She would phrase her thoughts to him with such words as, "What do you think?" or, "I just know you can figure it out," or, "I have such confidence in you."

Praising her husband did indeed have the desired effect. Most of her ideas were implemented and brought to practical reality by the hard work of her husband. At the completion of each new project, she would say something like, "I'm so proud of you, sweetheart. You do such good work. I just don't know what I would ever do without you."

Adam made an ax by fastening a sharp stone to a stick with leather thongs. He could chop and shape wood with it. By making wooden boxes and packing mud in them, then letting them dry in the sun, he could make bricks the same size and shape.

The woman helped with the work as much as she could, stopping now and then to rest. Adam carried food and water to her and sometimes stopped to rest with her and discuss the dimensions of the house.

It would be a large room with a door big enough to walk through without bending over. The walls would be made by stacking the clay bricks on top of each other. The roof would have to be made another way because they could not figure how to use bricks and make them stay overhead without falling down.

When the walls were completed, Adam had a great idea. He chopped down some trees about six or eight inches in diameter and trimmed them to make logs. He then laid them side by side across the top of the walls. Mud was then put on top of the logs to seal the roof.

After several weeks of hard work, the house was finished and they moved in. There was a raised portion along one inside wall where they could put things, instead of having everything on the floor.

Adam made a large basket in which to lay the baby. His wife wove many threads together to make soft cloths for the basket and the baby.

When he saw the linen threads she had spun, Adam brought woolen fibers he had cut from a sheep. He thought she might be able to make threads from that also. She was and she did.

One day, while she was spinning thread outside, near the door of their house, it happened. Adam was a short distance away, constructing a new and larger table to be used inside the house. "Adam! Adam!" she cried, "Come here. Come here."

Running quickly to her, he asked, "What's wrong?"

"Oh, Adam," she wailed. "I hurt...I hurt so bad." She asked him to help her get inside to lie down.

The pain subsided for a while and she rested a bit. "Adam," she said, "I think it is time for the little one to come out. I wonder if this is what God meant when He said I would have great pain in bearing children."

"I suppose so," replied Adam. "Is there anything I can do to help you?"

"Stay here with me," she said. "Just stay here with me."

After several hours of intermittent sieges of pain, she began to bear down and push with all her might. She was determined to force the baby out. At last, the head began to appear, but she could not push hard enough to make it come out.

"Adam," she panted, "please, please help me. I can't do it alone. Please help me, Adam."

He prayed, "God, help me. I don't know what to do."

Pressing here and there and trying to grasp the baby's head, he said, "Come on, honey, try to give one more great big push."

It worked. The baby came out. Adam picked it up and showed it to his wife. She smiled weakly.

The baby looked awful, blood and mucous all over. Adam looked at the baby and then at his wife. "Now, what should I do?" he asked.

Just then, three angels appeared. One was Adam's guardian angel. Another was his wife's and the third was being assigned to the child just born.

One of the angels spoke. "Adam, cut that little tube there. Then, tie a knot in it, close to the baby's belly. Wash the baby with water and give it to its mother. Also, clean up the residue there. Cleanliness is very important."

The angels disappeared, but stayed nearby to protect the family from any unauthorized attacks by Satan and his demons.

Chapter Seventeen

Invaded By Aliens

Satan, Baalmeg, Elgitlar and Pubilentre were keeping a close watch on earth's first family. They couldn't do much to harm them, though, because the guardian angels would only allow certain temptations and frustrations while the baby was small.

Several important discussions took place concerning long range plans to destroy the humans and defeat God's purpose for planet earth.

Elgitlar suggested that two of them survey the planet and estimate future population movements. High ranking demons should be assigned specific territories. They must train their troops to take every human being hostage. Not one human could be left alone to follow God. Satan agreed to do that as soon as an outline of overall plans could be formulated.

An evaluation of events thus far helped them to organize plans for the future. Pubilentre recounted, "You, Master, showed us how to tempt the first two humans there in the garden. We then turned them against each other by influencing their emotions and their pride.

"They immediately blamed each other for their own sin. Next, we got them to arguing and fighting, each one trying to be boss and make the decisions."

Pubilentre continued, "I particularly enjoyed watching him smash her face with his fists. Their guardian angels prevented us from motivating him to kill her, however. We've got to find a way to get past those guardian angels."

Baalmeg recalled Adam's encounter with the bear. "I almost got that bear to kill him. Do you think his guardian angel caused the dinosaur to attack the bear and rescue him?"

"Probably so," speculated Elgitlar. "Those angels are always messing up our plans. We need to make a deal with them to stand back once in a while and let us attack the humans."

"Hey! That's a great idea," exclaimed Satan. "Look, there are three of them, Adam, his wife and the baby. Now, here's the plan. I will get those three angels to take a walk with me. While I keep them busy discussing the matter, you three attack the humans.

"We can win this thing right here, near His precious garden. Ha, Ha, Haaaa. You kill the three of them and God will be defeated. His Garden of Eden will become a thicket of briars and brambles. Hee, Hee, Heeee. Oh, I am such a genius."

The four of them jumped up and walked hurriedly toward the first family's new house, excitedly plotting as they went.

Pubilentre said, "I shall squeeze Adam's heart until it stops beating. He will fall to the ground, gasping his last breath. I think I'll have him die right there in the house where she can watch it happen."

Baalmeg boasted, "Listen to this. I will attack the womb that formed that baby. The happy mother will suffer a postpartum hemorrhage. Heh, Heh, Heh. God shed the blood of innocent animals to cover their naked bodies. Now, she will die in a pool of her own sinful blood. Hey, Elgitlar, can you top that?"

Elgitlar smirked and said, "The baby will have no one to feed and care for it. Those angels don't have breast milk.

"The baby is too young for an animal to nurse it. The angels will just have to stand helplessly by and watch it starve to death. Oh, what agony. We shall taunt those angels. We shall watch their pious faces reflect the agony of defeat. We win, we win."

As they approached the house, the three generals hid behind some rocks while Satan proceeded.

The man and woman could not hear the conversation that was about to take place in the spirit realm.

Adam's angel was sitting just outside the front door, humming a tune that Satan recognized as a song he himself had composed long ago. The other two angels were over by the hot spring, discussing the pressures and heat that caused the spring water to be hot.

Satan approached Adam's angel and said, "Hello there. How are things going today?"

"All right," was the reply.

"My name is Satan, what's yours?"

The angel answered, "None of your business. What are you up to, anyway?"

"My! Aren't we testy today?" snarled Satan.

The angel stood up and drew his sword.

Satan backed up a step, held up his hands and said, "Let's don't get violent now. I just came to talk to you about something that might make your job a little easier. I tell you what, let's go get your friends over there by the hot spring and take a walk. I'll explain what I have in mind."

The angel replied, "I was told to not argue with you or rail against you, but I am free to use my sword if you try to do anything God has not authorized you to do. Now, you just turn around, go get your demon generals over there behind those rocks and go back to where you came from."

"How dare you talk to me like that?" growled Satan. "I

shall find a way to punish you for your obstinate attitude and your disrespectful mouth."

The angel raised his sword.

"You wouldn't dare," sneered Satan.

The sword slashed downward with the speed of light. Satan's dark uniform was sliced from top to bottom. His chest and stomach were cut by the point of the sword.

NOTE: How a disembodied spirit can wear clothing or be cut with a sword is not known. The author just reports what he sees in the visions. It is well to remember that much of what is seen in visions is symbolic and is not to be taken too literally.

The humiliated Devil glared at the angel and through clenched teeth snarled, "You'll pay for this." He turned and stomped away, cursing furiously.

Gathering his generals, he retreated a safe distance away. "Well, I guess we'll have to figure something else out," he told them.

Satan became more gloomy and hateful. Sometimes he would not even lead the discussions. Other times he'd explode in a rage and curse the generals.

During one of those discussions, Pubilentre said, "Do you suppose that baby inherited the sin of its parents?"

"I think it did," replied Elgitlar. "It came out of them and is a part of them. Surely it was born in sin. I don't see how it could be any other way."

Baalmeg disagreed, "God wouldn't throw that baby into eternal fire. It can't talk. It can't think. It can't make any kind of decision. It doesn't know right from wrong."

"Oh, shut up and stop your preaching," shouted Satan. "God said you are going to burn in the fire forever and what did you ever do wrong? Answer me that if you can."

Baalmeg's eyes narrowed and his mouth tightened as he answered, "I made a conscious choice to forsake God and follow you."

Satan roared. He cursed and screamed at Baalmeg. "You fool! You dumb, stupid, idiotic fool. I am assigning you to personally see to it that the baby sins as soon as it is old enough to think. I am not taking any chances. Do you understand?"

"Yes Master," said Baalmeg, cowering before the one who would become known as the god of this world.

In the weeks and months that followed, Baalmeg made frequent visits to the little family, looking for the first opportunity to tempt the baby to sin. He found that he could wake the baby frequently and cause it to cry loudly, frustrating both the mother and father and depriving them of sleep.

The three guardian angels made no attempt to stop Baalmeg's disruptive efforts. They only would not allow him to directly attack. He found that he could communicate his subtle temptations and influence to the parents' minds without them even realizing who he was or what he was doing to them.

"I am so tired of being up several times a night to care for this baby," said the mother.

Adam agreed, "Yeah, and I'm sick of washing all those diaper cloths. I wonder how long this is going to go on?"

"I don't know," replied the woman, "but I sure could use some rest from it all."

The man said, "Let's wait a while before we have any more babies."

"If it's this bad with every one," remarked the woman, "I don't know if I ever want another one."

160

"Well," replied Adam, "God told us to be fruitful and multiply. When this baby gets big enough to walk, maybe it won't be so difficult."

Baalmeg made reports to Satan, keeping him advised about the trouble and frustration he was causing earth's first family.

Pubilentre and Satan left Elgitlar and Baalmeg to harass the humans and took off to map the planet and organize plans and strategies, just in case the little family should happen to multiply.

While they were flying over the surface of the earth, Satan and Pubilentre prioritized their goals. "What we need to do," said Pubilentre, "is find a way to kill them before they have more children."

"We've already tried that," replied Satan. "However, we must keep on trying. That must be our first priority."

Pubilentre queried, "Suppose the guardian angels keep them so well protected that we cannot kill them?"

"Then we shall develop other plans," answered Satan. "We must make sure that every human sins and falls under the condemnation of fire. That is the only chance we have to defeat God and force Him to free us. We must not fail."

"Hey! I've got an idea," shouted Pubilentre. "Let's get them to kill each other."

"That's a good idea," responded Satan, "but I don't think it will work. Those guardian angels can speak to the human soul as well as we can. Let's keep that in mind, though. Maybe we can do some damage there."

When the survey of the planet was completed, Satan and Pubilentre returned to Eridu, where Adam built his first house and would later build the world's first city. They rested and shared with Elgitlar and Baalmeg what they had learned from their trip around the world.

Little did Satan realize that a thousand years later he would be making daily trips around the world, checking on his generals and directing a massive war against hundreds of millions of humans.

Satan decided it was time to bring all of the fallen angels to earth. He issued an order that would affect the life of every human that would ever be born. "Pubilentre," he commanded, "go back to our camp and bring all of our troops here. We must make this planet ours. We cannot let these humans have dominion here."

Pubilentre left at once, knowing it would take a while to accomplish the task. He knew that by this time many of the fallen angels would no longer want to follow Satan and be bullied by him. It would not be easy to get them all to come to earth.

On the long trip to the camp he organized his thoughts to be most effective because he knew Satan would punish him severely if even one angel escaped his control.

Arriving there, he was greeted enthusiastically by some of the officers. Most of the common troops, however, simply wished he had never returned. They were comfortable going about their affairs without the awful interruptions and ridiculous orders from Lucifer upsetting them.

Pubilentre called a meeting of the commanders to convey Satan's orders to them. He spoke glowingly of his Master's skill in causing the first two humans to fall into sin and of his taking the title deed to the earth.

"It will be our kingdom" he assured them. "We will rule over the earth and all of its inhabitants. We must give our total energy and effort to helping our Master thwart God's purpose on that little planet. Our only hope of escaping the eternal lake of fire is to defeat God and force Him to rescind His judgment against us.

"I don't believe God would create those humans, let us tempt them into sin and then just throw them all into the fire with us. He may be severe, but He is never unjust. We must not allow one human to escape from sin and judgment. Do you understand me? Not one.

"Furthermore, we must not allow one of our troops to remain here. You must make sure that every angel goes to earth with us. You must frighten them into obeying you. You must not fail."

Meetings were organized throughout the camp and fear was preached until the terrified angels were begging to go to earth. They were accounted for by districts, sections and divisions and prepared for the long journey. Any thoughts of desertion were eradicated by threats of the most awful punishments imaginable.

Moving twelve billion horrified angels took more time than when Satan and the three generals made the trip. It was accomplished, though, and Satan, Baalmeg and Elgitlar were waiting to greet them when they arrived.

A mass meeting was held and Satan himself addressed the crowd. "Welcome to you new home," he roared. "This is our kingdom. We will rule this planet and defeat the Almighty's puny experiment.

"I am promoting many of you to higher ranks. Some of you will be generals. Many commanders will become captains. More lieutenants will be commanders. A host of other promotions from among the ranks will be added.

"We must occupy every square inch of this planet. We must make sure every human is damned to the fire. The first couple has already produced a child. There may be more, many more.

"There are twelve billion of us. We must create such

mayhem, murder and destruction that it will take thousands of years to fill the earth with humans.

"As soon as that first child was born, a guardian angel was assigned to protect him. As each new human is born, one of you will be assigned to tempt him into sin. It will be your job to destroy him.

"It is vital that not one human escapes us. I am going to be perfectly frank with you. If we fail, we will burn forever in the lake of fire. Our only chance to avoid the fire is to defeat God through these humans and force Him to free us.

"Commanders, get your troops settled in temporary quarters. Pubilentre, Baalmeg and Elgitlar, come with me. We must discuss promotions and assign territories. A strict order of business must be drawn up and implemented immediately."

Satan listened to suggestions for promotions, personally interviewed each candidate and approved the changes. When all was decided, a huge parade was organized and the promotions were made with great fanfare. Specific assignments were then given.

Twelve generals were given large territories to rule over. Some of them would later be given additional titles because of their strategic importance in certain areas of the world. Those extra titles would include "Principality," "Power," "Ruler of Darkness."

Pubilentre, Baalmeg and Elgitlar were promoted and given special rank. They were called "Elqandea," which means "the god who knows how to obtain results." They were kept close to Satan and helped him administrate the affairs of the entire Kingdom of Darkness. They could speak on Satan's behalf and could give direct orders to even the highest ranking generals.

Satan spent some time praising and encouraging the

generals, captains and commanders in their new jobs. That didn't last long, though, for as soon as some of them began to fail in their assignments, or be defeated by guardian angels, he reverted back to yelling, screaming, cursing and threatening.

The three elqandeas and Satan took personal charge of the small area around Eridu, so they could show the territorial rulers how to enslave humans and blind them to the knowledge of Almighty God.

Adam and his wife would prove to be extremely difficult, because they had spoken directly with God and would be suspicious of any endeavor to get them to worship anyone else. It was decided that Baalmeg would be given all the help, advice and assistance he needed to corrupt and destroy the first baby.

Sentinels were posted day and night to monitor every aspect of the baby's development. Reports were carefully made and reviewed to try to determine just when the child could make his first conscious choice between good and evil, between right and wrong.

Generals were invited to view the demonic influences on the first family at close range. Lectures were given to inform them of the latest discoveries.

Later, a meeting of the captains was held near Eridu to acquaint them more fully with the first family. Strengths and weaknesses of each human were discussed and suggestions made as to how to draw them away from God and into the bondage of sin.

Chapter Eighteen

Am I My Brother's Guardian?

While Satan and his fallen angels were organizing and plotting the destruction of the human race, Adam and his wife were busy caring for the new life they had brought into the world.

Adam named his wife Eve, which means "life giver," because she would be the first mother to every person that would ever be born.

Eve named the newborn son Cain, meaning "created," for she said, "God has helped me create this child."

The first year was difficult for the little family. Eve spent most of her time caring for the baby. Adam had to do all of his regular work and also those things that Eve could not do because of baby Cain.

After that, things got a little better. Eve was able to help her husband with some of the outside work. Adam planted a garden near the house so they would not have to search for wild vegetables. He planted fruit trees and bushes nearby, as well as a vineyard.

How did Adam learn to do those things? He prayed for wisdom and knowledge. God spoke to him and gave specific instructions on some things, but let Adam figure others out for himself.

As Cain grew and matured, he began helping his mother with chores around the house. His help was greatly needed because Eve was giving birth to more children about every two years: Abel, a brother; Yarah, a sister; Erek, a brother; Lulu, a sister.

The next child after Lulu was a girl whom they named Mattanel. Then Eve bore twin boys. That kept everybody busy for about a year. After that, two girls, then three boys and five more girls.

Eve was strong and was a very good mother, keeping the older children busy with chores while she nursed the newest members of the family.

When Cain was six he began helping his father with the garden, the vineyard and the orchard. He also learned to domesticate and care for animals, but he much preferred the soil to all those smelly beasts.

Adam added rooms to the house to accommodate the growing family. He planted more fruit and nut trees, more vines and berry bushes. The garden was enlarged and new ways to till the ground were sought.

Digging the ground with a stick was more work than he and Cain could do with so large a garden. One day Cain suggested they sharpen a large tree branch, get some long leather strips and tie them to an animal. They could have the animal pull the branch and the sharp point would dig up the ground much faster than they could ever do it by hand.

After some adjustments, they found they could plow a much larger garden. The animal they used to pull the plow was an ox.

When Cain was full grown, his parents gave him the oldest girl to be his wife. Her name was Yarah, or "teacher." A great party was held in honor of this marriage. There was much singing and dancing. Adam told Cain and Yarah some of the things God had revealed to him in the Garden of Eden.

Cain built a house in a little valley about two miles from his father's house. He planted a garden and raised a bountiful crop of vegetables. He had only a few animals and gave most of his time to gardening.

Yarah worked hard to prepare their home for children, but she had a sickness for several years that prevented her from bearing children.

Adam had carefully instructed all of his children to be thankful to God for everything they had. They were taught how to offer sacrifices to God.

In those early days, a fat, healthy lamb would be prepared and laid upon a stone altar. The one offering it would then back away a few paces, bow down, pray and wait.

If the worshiper's heart was sincere and if the sacrifice had been properly selected and prepared, God would send fire down from heaven and consume it.

Cain one day watched his brother Abel preparing a lamb for sacrifice. Adam had told all of his family that harvest time was a good time to be thankful to God for the increase of herds and flocks and crops.

Abel was taking great care to make sure the lamb was perfect and that the preparing of it was done exactly as Adam had instructed. Cain watched his brother with contempt.

Adam and Eve had always lavished extra attention upon Abel because he had been born weak and sickly. They named him Abel, which means "temporary" because they thought he might die in infancy. He had always been given lighter chores, while Cain was expected to carry the heavy loads.

Cain hated his brother. Abel had been such a "mama's boy" from the beginning, always obeying every little request cheerfully. It was disgusting.

Adam would hold the little creep on his lap and tell him what a fine boy he was. His mother would boil brothy soup and herbal tea just for him. Cain, on the other hand, would be told to hurry up and finish the heavy chores while mom and dad fawned over the poor little sick thing.

Abel became stronger as he grew to manhood and was beginning to raise sheep and cattle. He had recently married Lulu and was given a much bigger and more lavish wedding than Cain and Yarah had received. A huge farm was allotted to Abel for the flocks and herds he would be raising.

Now, he was sacrificing the choicest lamb from his small but growing flock. Cain watched the whole ritual from a short distance away, sitting on a rock, resting from his labors in his own large garden.

Abel's sacrifice was accepted. Fire came down and burned it up. Abel worshiped until it was entirely consumed and then got up and returned to his home.

Cain knew he did not have an acceptable lamb. The only one under a year old had a broken leg. Two sickly ewes and one scruffy old ram couldn't produce much for sacrifice. Why wouldn't some vegetables and grain do just as well?

He certainly was not going to his brother and purchase a lamb from him. He wouldn't go to Adam and request one either. He didn't want to hear the lecture he would get on being diligent in raising acceptable animals just to sacrifice them to some invisible God.

Cain gathered fruits, vegetables and grain and brought them to the altar that Abel had constructed. He couldn't see any point in building a new one himself.

Piling the food on top of the still warm altar, he backed away and bowed down, keeping his eyes on the altar to watch the fire come down.

Nothing happened. No fire. He waited. Maybe God

was busy and would send the fire in a few moments. He waited. Still nothing.

Several birds came, landed on top of the vegetables and began eating the grain. Cain felt rejected and angry. Why wouldn't the labor of his hands be just as acceptable as the blood of an animal?

Oh, yes, he had heard of the fig leaves in Eden and the animal skins for clothing, but it just didn't make sense.

Cain left the food lying there on the altar and returned home. His face was clouded with anger as he entered the house.

"What's wrong?" his wife asked.

"Shut up!" he shouted, striking her and slamming her against the wall. He turned and stomped out of the house and went for a long walk.

He sat down near where the river flowed into the gulf and rehearsed in his mind all the things he hated about his brother. If only his brother hadn't been born. If only his brother hadn't been sick. If only his brother hadn't been such a little nice guy.

Cain formulated a plan. He would get rid of his brother. He would then speak to Adam and offer to take responsibility for his brother's ranch. That would give him plenty of fine lambs for sacrifice.

Oh, yes, his brother's wife. She was just a child when Cain married Yarah. Yarah hadn't borne any children yet and she was getting to be such a nag. She wanted children and somehow she was blaming him. "How could it be my fault?" he grumbled to himself.

Abel's wife, Lulu, was all grown up now, very pretty, very desirable. "I'll bet she could bear lots of beautiful children for me," Cain said out loud. "Lulu," he continued, "her name means 'if only, if only.' That's right, if only I had waited and married her instead of Yarah."

Cain rose and walked toward home. As he walked, he planned the details of what he was going to do. The brother he hated would be gone forever and he would get all of his brother's possessions, including that beautiful young wife.

About halfway home, Cain stopped to rest. He washed his face in the cool waters of a small stream, took a long refreshing drink and sat down under a tree.

"Cain...Cain," a voice called. He had never heard that voice before. It sounded like it came out of nowhere, yet everywhere. He looked up in the tree to see if someone was up there, then all around, but saw no one.

The voice spoke again, "Cain, why are you so angry? Your face looks dark and sullen. If you would only obey, your face could wear a happy smile. However, if you refuse, be on your guard, because sin is lurking nearby and it wants to devour you.

"You don't have to let sin rule over you. If you will just listen and obey, you can conquer sin."

Without a word, Cain ran from that place. He reasoned that what he heard was the voice of God that Adam had told him about. He didn't want to hear it. It might convince him to change his plans.

He ran about a quarter of a mile. Not hearing the voice anymore, he slowed to a walk and continued planning how he was going to do away with his brother.

Cain arrived home demanding that his wife fix him something to eat and refusing all questions about where he had been.

Several days later, Cain went over to Abel's house and said, "Let's take a walk. I have something I want to discuss with you. Let's go to the meadow that has those large rocks jutting up out of the ground."

It was about five miles to the place and when they got there, Cain said, "Let's sit down here and rest."

As Abel sat down, Cain picked up a rock and smashed it against his brother's head. Abel fell over, unconscious. Cain pounded him again and again with the rock until his own hands, arms and clothing were spattered with blood. Abel was dead.

Finding a dry limb from a tree, Cain managed to dig a grave. He put his brother's body in and covered it with dirt. Wanting to be sure no one would discover it, he camouflaged the grave with rocks and leaves.

He went to the river and bathed thoroughly, washing his clothes and drying them in the sun. He went home convinced that no one would ever know.

Cain would soon learn a lesson that should be taught to every child---there is no such thing as a secret. Oh, what misery could be spared if only that lesson was part of every child's education.

The next day, Lulu came over and asked, "Where is Abel? He went out with you but he never came back. Where is he?"

Cain answered, "He said he wanted to explore the other side of the river. He swam across and walked northeast from there. That's the last I saw of him."

"Why didn't you come and tell me?" said Lulu. "I have been sick with worry about him. If anything happens to him I shall hold you personally responsible." She turned and walked away, weeping as she went.

The next few days were uneasy for Cain. Adam inquired about Abel and so did several others. Cain gave them all the same answer. A search party went looking for Abel without success. It was concluded that wild animals must have eaten him. Forty days of grieving helped them accept the loss.

After what seemed an appropriate amount of time, Cain visited Adam and offered to assume ownership of Abel's flocks and herds, his house and his wife.

"Do you realize," said Adam, "that any children Lulu bears will be your total responsibility to raise and provide for? And do you know that you must keep the two estates separate so that her children can inherit Abel's property when they come of age?

"Do you understand that her children will bear his name, not yours? You will be fully responsible for them, but you will have no claim on them or anything that is theirs."

Cain thought about that for a moment. In his own mind he figured he could work his way around the conditions his autocratic father was demanding. Besides, his lust for the beautiful Lulu influenced his reasoning.

"I am prepared to do whatever I can for the memory of my dear brother," he said, looking straight into the face of Adam and smiling convincingly.

Adam sent Erek to call Lulu. She came immediately. "Lulu," he said, "Cain has offered to care for you and all of your possessions. He has agreed to give you children in your husband's name. Will you marry him and let him provide for you and keep Abel's name from disappearing from the earth?"

"No!" screamed Lulu, "I wouldn't marry Cain if you gave me the whole world and everything in it. I wouldn't trust him with a broken thong from my shoe. I certainly would not give my body to him. I would rather die than join myself to him.

"If a brother doesn't ask for me, then I shall go to my grave a widow and my husband's name will vanish from the earth."

She stormed out of the house in a fit of rage, shouting to those gathered outside, "I'll bet he knows what happened to my husband and I'll bet he is responsible."

As Cain walked toward his home, he said to himself, "What did I ever see in her? She is not nearly so pretty as I thought she was. Oh, well, I wonder what would happen if Mattanel's husband was to die? Her name means 'gift of God' and I just imagine she would be a real gift. Yeah, a real gift."

He had just passed over the top of a hill and was descending to the valley where he lived. He could see his house in the distance.

Suddenly, he heard that voice again, the voice he did not want to hear.

"Cain."

He walked on, pretending not to hear. His eyes looked toward the ground. His steps quickened.

The voice spoke again. "Cain!" This time it was loud and commanding.

He stopped. He didn't look up, but continued looking down at the ground.

"Cain," the voice said, "where is your brother Abel?"

Cain hesitated just a second or two and then answered, "I don't know where he is. I don't keep a record where he goes or what he does."

Again that voice of authority filled the air and said, "Cain, I want you to tell Me where your brother is."

Cain felt blood rush to his face with such pressure he thought he would faint. He blinked his eyes, turned his head from side to side and moved his shoulders because the muscles were becoming tense.

His answer would be used as an excuse by countless generations of men after him. "Am I my brother's guardian? Am I responsible to take care of him? Come on, give me a break. I take care of myself. Let him take care of himself."

God patiently listened while Cain tried to avoid telling the truth and asking for mercy. Then, God spoke with a voice filled with grief and pity, because He knew the future and the awful consequences of Cain's mindset and rebellion.

He said, "Cain, your brother's blood is crying to Me from the ground. Please tell Me what you have done."

Silence.

God continued, "Cain, My son, I could not accept your sacrifice because your heart was not right. You refused to obey the clear instructions of your father Adam. And now, you are standing here lying to Me.

"Please, Cain, admit your sin. Take your punishment like a man. Seek forgiveness and pledge yourself to listen carefully to My laws and obey Me to the best of your ability."

Cain didn't move. He didn't look up. He clenched his teeth behind tightly pursed lips and tried to slow his breathing in an effort to calm his racing emotions. It was a dreadful moment of silence.

God's voice sadly spoke the judgment. "You have defiled the ground with your brother's blood. From now on, the ground will not respond to you. When you plant crops they will not grow. The very ground will resist you. It will not produce a harvest for you, no matter how hard you work or how much you plant.

"From this day on, you will wander over the face of the earth as a fugitive."

"A fugitive?" said Cain. "How can I be a fugitive? Nobody knows what happened."

God answered, "Cain, there is no such thing as a secret. If only you would learn that lesson, you could spare yourself much grief.

"Tomorrow, your brother Chema, whose name means 'hot displeasure and indignation,' will be hunting with his dog Belaqar, whose name means 'to discover that which was destroyed,' and the dog will sniff out your awful deed.

"Chema will tell everyone and show them your brother's remains. They will go to Adam and demand justice. You will be tried and found guilty of murder. Since you refuse to acknowledge your sin and ask for forgiveness, your only hope to survive is to run far away."

Cain stiffened and turned his eyes upward to see if he could see the God who was speaking to him. He saw nothing. He had no respect for a God who wouldn't even show Himself, a God who was more demanding and unfair than his father Adam. Hot tears formed in his eyes and his voice spoke bitterly.

"Your judgment against me is more than I can bear. You are totally unfair to me, just like Adam has always been. You are driving me away from my land. You are casting me out like garbage.

"If You wouldn't let them find him, they would never know. You are making me a fugitive and a wanderer. They will surely find me and when they kill me it will be Your fault."

God sounded sad, but kind and gentle. "Cain, My son, please understand, I don't hate you. I love you and I want the very best for you. I will speak to Adam and tell him to notify everyone in the family not to kill you.

"I will put an identifying mark on you to warn everyone who sees you not to harm you. If anyone does kill you, his punishment will be seven times more severe than yours.

176

"Cain, I want you to go far away and make a new start. Change your stubborn way of thinking and be obedient to My laws. You are the first-born of Adam. When he dies, you can become the head of the family and teach them My laws. You can lead them in the pathway of righteousness.

"I would rather have your loving obedience than any sacrifice you can offer Me. Please, Cain, I want you to…"

Cain wouldn't listen to another word. He ran down the hill and across the field to his house.

"Pack some things, whatever you can carry," he shouted to his wife. "I'll take some food and wine. We are leaving this place and going away."

"Why?" asked Yarah. "I like this place just fine."

"Don't argue with me," he growled. "Get busy."

Yarah pleaded, "Can't we wait until morning? We haven't even had supper yet."

"No, we can't," he answered. "We must cross the river early tomorrow. Come on, now, let's go."

Chapter Nineteen

Nod, Land Of Wandering

Baalmeg reported to Satan, "Master, I have done it. I got Cain to kill one of his brothers. Now, he is running away to escape the wrath of his family. He and his wife are going to cross the river tomorrow. Shall I drown them both? We can stop one whole line of Adam's descendants right here."

"No," replied Satan. "With them separated from the Godly influence of Adam, they can raise a family of killers. After they are strong, they can kill all the families of Adam and then kill each other. We will be victorious. We will defeat God by destroying every human."

Baalmeg said, "But Master, Cain's wife cannot bear children. How can we raise murderers that way?"

"That will be your problem," retorted Satan. "If his wife remains barren, you must get him another wife. I leave the details to you."

Late that evening, Cain and his wife arrived at the river's edge. They ate some of the food Cain had carried from the house. Yarah unfolded a blanket and spread it on the ground for them to sleep on.

The moon was nearly full and sparkled in the gently flowing water of the river. An owl sat in a nearby tree, watching the couple as they prepared to sleep.

As they lay there in the semi-darkness, their minds were uneasy and their hearts were disturbed by the emotions swirling in their breasts.

Yarah waited for Cain to speak. He said nothing. She

could feel the tension emanating from her husband. After a few moments of silence she asked, "Why are we leaving our home, our garden and all that we have obtained there? And what is that mark on your forehead? I noticed it when you came into the house today. Did you hurt yourself?"

Cain looked at her and saw only sincere questions in her eyes. They seemed non-threatening and not at all judgmental. He decided to tell her everything.

"I killed that righteous little wimp Abel. He was always so perfect in spirit and so imperfect in body. I did all the heavy work and he got all the praise for the little he did."

Yarah commented, "He was not strong enough to do all the great things you do. He could never accomplish the mighty tasks you perform. You are so strong and he was so weak. You should never be jealous of him."

"That's true," replied Cain, "but everyone always approved of him and nobody ever so much as said 'thanks' to me for all my hard work."

"Well, I appreciate your great strength and your hard work," assured Yarah. "My only disappointment is that you have not given me children."

Cain responded, "Hey! I don't think that is my fault. Remember, you are the one who has the sickness. If I had another wife, I might have several children by now."

"You're probably right," agreed Yarah. "This sick body of mine just cannot make babies. Maybe you should have another wife to give you children."

Her husband complained, "You know, it just seems that everyone and everything is against me. Even God is against me. He made you sick so you cannot bear children for me. He accepted the bloody sacrifice from that 'Oh, so perfect' brother of mine and rejected the labor of my hands.

"Now, God has turned my family against me. He is

179

going to let Chema and his dog Belaqar find Abel's body and go tell everybody what I did. They will come looking for me to kill me. That's why we must flee across the river."

"We will establish our own family, our own city and our own tribe. We don't need them. We don't need their rules, their revenge, their righteous indignation. We can get along just fine without them.

"The mark on my forehead? God put it there to warn them not to kill me. He said that if anyone does kill me, his punishment will be seven times more severe than mine."

Yarah consoled him with, "You're right, my husband. I will go with you wherever you go. I will surely have children someday and I will teach them to obey you and follow your example.

"We will raise up a strong family. We will establish our own rules. We will live the way we want to and if they ever find us or bother us, we will kill all of them."

"All right," said Cain. "We will find a good place far away from them and build a great home. If you cannot have any children, I will sneak back across the river and kidnap one of the healthy young girls.

"She will be our slave. All of the children she bears will be yours. Our family records will show you as their mother."

"That's very good," agreed Yarah. "Let's go to sleep now. We have a lot of work to do tomorrow."

They rose early the next morning and finished eating the food they had brought with them. The blanket, some clothing and a few other things were all they had been able to carry from their house, but they proved to be too much to cross the river with.

"How are we going to get across?" inquired Yarah.

"The water is deep and we cannot swim and carry all these things. What shall we do?"

Cain replied, "See those two small trees over there? We shall cut them down, tie them together, put our things on them and float across the river."

He found a sharp stone, fastened it to a dry branch and began chopping. Before long, they had a primitive raft ready to launch.

They put their belongings on the raft and pushed it out into the river, swimming alongside to guide it across. However, the current swept them downstream into the gulf.

For several hours they struggled until finally they reached the other side of the gulf. Exhausted, they unloaded their things and set up camp right there at the water's edge. A few berries were all they could find to eat.

The next day they packed up and began to walk north. "How far do you think we should go?" asked Yarah.

"Well, we need to go far enough so they cannot find us," replied Cain.

After a journey of two days, Yarah said, "This looks like a good place. Let's make our home here. See the pleasant stream and the fruit trees?"

"No," said Cain. "We need to go farther. We are still too close to Eridu."

"But that is way on the other side of the river," reasoned Yarah. "They won't find us here."

"This is only a couple of days journey from there," answered Cain. "Come on, we've got to go farther."

Two more days of walking exhausted Yarah. When they stopped to rest, she said, "I'm not going another step. I'm going to stay right here."

Cain surveyed the area and saw that it looked like a good place to live and raise a family. "Okay," he said, "we'll stay here."

Fruits, nuts and vegetables were plentiful. They killed several animals and used the skins to make a tent. A stone or brick house might be considered later.

They planted a large garden and waited for it to grow. Hardly anything sprouted and what did sprout did not develop into mature produce.

"I wonder why the food we planted won't grow here," said Yarah. "We had such a wonderful garden back home. You are such an expert gardener. The wild fruits and vegetables here seem to grow all right. It is just our garden that won't grow."

Cain explained, "God told me that because I defiled the ground with my brother's blood, the ground would no longer respond to me. He said that no matter how hard I work or how much I plant, the ground will not produce a harvest for me."

"What are we going to do?" inquired Yarah. "The wild fruits and vegetables around here won't last forever."

"Well," replied Cain, "when the food here runs out, we will just move somewhere else. If we can no longer get food to grow for us, we will simply go and find new sources of food. It's a big world out there and I'm sure we can find plenty to eat."

After about a year, the wild food diminished. Cain searched farther and farther to find enough food to sustain them. One day he came home and announced that he had found a beautiful valley about fifteen miles away that had an abundance of food growing there.

Since they had been living in a tent and had not obtained very many things, it was easy for them to pack up and move. They loaded their possessions onto two donkeys and journeyed to the new valley.

"Are we going to keep moving like this every time food

gets scarce?" asked Yarah. "Maybe when we kill an animal for its skin we could eat its flesh. What do you think?"

"I don't know," replied her husband. "We might die if we eat the flesh of an animal."

Yarah reasoned, "We have seen wild animals killing and eating each other. We even have to guard ourselves so they don't eat us. I think it is worth a try."

"No," responded Cain. "It might poison us. Do you remember Adam telling us that some plants are poison and we cannot eat them? Maybe animal flesh is also poison and we would die if we ate it.

"I'll tell you what," he continued. "I will go back across the river and capture one of the girls to be our slave. She will bear a child for us. When it is old enough to eat solid food, we will kill an animal and give some of its flesh to the child. If it dies we will know we cannot eat animal flesh."

Yarah looked straight into her husband's eyes and said, "That is the most disgusting thing I have ever heard. Would you sacrifice the life of your own child for an experiment like that?"

Cain replied, "Why not? Our slave girl could bear more children for us."

Yarah said, "If I ever have a child and you do anything like that, I will cut your heart out and feed it to the birds. My children will not be used for any experiments."

About three months later, a family of dinosaurs moved into the area and began devouring the vegetation. Yarah was terrified by the giant creatures. "Let's move away from here," she demanded.

"No," said her husband. "The dinosaurs will move on soon. They won't be here long."

"I'm afraid," she responded. "Those monsters may eat

us. They might rip our tent to shreds in the night and kill us before we have a chance to run."

Cain reasoned, "They only eat vegetation. They won't bother us at all."

"You can stay here if you want to," said Yarah. "I am packing up and leaving right now."

He decided that he might as well go. His wife was a good cook, even if she was a nag. They were soon on their way north and east.

They found a broad plain near the Tigris River and settled there. Although there were many animals, they were well fed and did not seem hostile toward the humans.

Cain and his wife moved whenever food became scarce or when aggressive animals invaded the area.

Eventually, they found a place where they felt they could build a house of sun-dried bricks and stay for a long time. It was a large house and they filled it with furniture and dishes and clothing they made.

"At last," said Yarah, "we won't have to call this country 'Nod, the land of wandering.' Now, we have found a permanent home."

"That's right," agreed Cain. "Here is where I will build my first city."

Chapter Twenty

Queen Of Enochtown

Yarah's health improved and she became pregnant. Cain busied himself preparing the house for the arrival of the baby, while Yarah spun soft cloth for the tiny one. A large basket was woven from reeds for the baby to sleep in. Yarah even managed to make a sheer covering to put over the basket to protect the baby from flies and other insects.

When the baby was born they named him Enoch. He was a strong baby and developed a terrible temper. Yarah exhausted herself caring for the rambunctious child. Cain was proud of the strong-willed boy who was so much like himself.

As the years passed, other children were born until Yarah became sick again and could no longer conceive. Cain decided to keep his children and grandchildren close by so he could establish a city from which he could govern the tribe.

He named the city "Enoch" after his firstborn son instead of after himself. He did not want the "Mark of Cain" to be associated with the city and his descendants.

Cain hoped to be the father of several tribes or nations. His wife, however, had not borne a child in ten years. He felt he must find a way to increase his family. Maybe Enoch could have two wives and lots of children.

The two oldest daughters were given to Enoch in a wild drunken ceremony. Enoch feasted and drank to such excess that he could not consummate his marriage to the girls for six days. Yarah vented her rage on Cain for making such a debauchery of marriage.

Within a year, Enoch's wives were pregnant, but both of them had violent miscarriages and nearly died. Enoch blamed his father and mother for not providing better food for the girls.

Cain spoke to Enoch's younger brother and said, "Elchan, I am going to give your sisters, Maladar and Eshpalan, to you in marriage. I want you to give me many grandchildren."

"But father, I am only fifteen years old," argued Elchan. "How can I raise a family and provide for them? I am too young. Please let me wait a few years. And besides, Maladar and Eshpalan are older than me. I'd rather wait and marry one of the younger girls."

His father replied, "You're going to do it now. I must have a greater increase in this family now. At this time you and Enoch are my only sons. You must give me grandchildren soon."

This wedding was not as boisterous as the former one. Elchan built a crude hut not far from Cain's house and after about a year the girls were pregnant.

The three remaining girls were twelve, fourteen and fifteen years old. There were no sons of Cain for them to marry. Yarah still could not conceive.

One day Yarah and the three girls were out gathering wild vegetables, fruits, nuts and berries. The girls were eating more than they were putting into their baskets.

Yarah looked at them and said, "Girls, you have all been eating too much food lately. You're gaining weight. Look at you. Your tummies are sticking out."

A dreadful thought struck her mind. "Girls, how long has it been since the way of women has happened?"

The girls were silent for a moment. It was Pilinidneh

186

who spoke first. "Mother, we have something to tell you. Our father has been raping us for several months. We are all pregnant."

"Why didn't you tell me?" screamed their horrified mother. "How could you let this happen?"

The girls spoke almost in unison, "He threatened to hurt us really bad if we told. We knew you'd find out sooner or later and we didn't want him to hurt us."

Yarah cried for a moment and then through tear stained eyes looked with compassion on her three daughters. "This isn't the way I wanted to raise a family," she said. "I guess I had too many girls and not enough boys. I'm sorry, girls. I'm sorry I couldn't have boys for you to marry."

They cried with their mother and consoled her. "It's not your fault, Mother. Maybe after our babies are weaned we can leave them with you for a while and go across the river to Adam's family and find husbands. We'll bring them here and give you lots of grandbabies."

"Oh, my darling girls," cried Yarah. "You are so precious to me. Promise me you will always stay close by me and raise your children where I can see them every day.

"My soul is torn with hatred for your father and love for my tiny grandchildren growing inside your bodies. I love you all. Please don't ever forsake me. I would die without your love and affection."

Cain made tents for each of the girls and equipped them with baskets for the babies. Yarah wove blankets and clothing and diapers.

As each baby was born, Cain would celebrate by getting drunk. He was not at all ashamed of himself. He boasted that he was obtaining offspring that Yarah could not provide. Yarah busied herself with the babies.

When Yarah refused Cain's sexual advances, he beat her

and raped her. He regularly raped the three girls and Enoch's wives when Enoch was out hunting. One day when Elchan was away, Cain raped his wives also.

They told Elchan about it when he returned. He confronted his father and said, "If you ever touch my wives again, I will enlist the help of my brother Enoch. We will tie you to that tree over there. We will then fetch our hunting dogs and gather the whole family to watch the dogs eat you alive."

Cain realized that his son meant exactly what he said. He decided to turn his attentions elsewhere. He made several trips across the river, returning each time with slaves. Three young men were provided for the three girls.

The whole family celebrated each wedding and helped the couples build houses of sun-dried bricks. The young men were pleased with the girls and did not try to escape. They worked hard to provide for the babies.

Cain brought six young girls across the river for himself. He enlarged his house and gave each girl a room of her own. The six of them together produced an average of two babies a year.

Yarah was considered the queen of Enochtown. She eventually began conceiving and bearing children again. Cain captured two more girls to be servants to her. By this time she needed a lot of help.

Cain kept all of the family close by to build his city as soon as possible. The people he captured from across the river found that they could plant crops and receive a bountiful harvest. Cain demanded that they give him food for his wives and children. He no longer even tried to grow food himself.

The city became crowded as his descendants multiplied. After about a hundred years they began to migrate and find suitable land where they could raise their rapidly growing families.

Cain lived seven hundred years, fathering a great many sons and daughters, creating several major families or tribes.

Enoch, the first son of Cain, had a son named Irad. He became the father of Mehujael. Mehujael was the father of Methusael, who had a son named Lamech. Now, Lamech had two wives, Adah and Zillah.

One of Adah's sons was named Jabal. His descendants lived in portable tents and raised cattle. They moved about with the cattle, searching for water and good grazing areas.

Adah named another of her sons Jubal. He invented the harp and the flute. How different brothers can be.

Lamech's other wife, Zillah, bore a son and named him Tubal-cain. He started a metalworking industry.

One day Lamech got into a fight with a teenager and killed him. He went home and spoke to his wives about it. "Look," he said, "a boy attacked me and wounded me. I struck back and killed him. His family will surely come looking for me.

"I don't think I should be put to death for that. As a matter of fact, if someone who kills Cain is punished seven times, I think anyone who kills me should be punished seventy-seven times."

Most of Cain's descendants did not worship God. They began to hear voices of demons in the trees, in rocks, in the streams of water and in animals.

Those who turn away from God, their Creator, will soon begin to worship other "gods" that Satan invents for them.

The road to hell was soon to become a broad and busy highway to eternal horror. Those who go there never return.

Chapter Twenty-One

Going To Hell

Satan and his twelve billion fallen angels had been on earth almost a hundred and fifty years. He had built a large palace for himself in the spirit realm above Eridu. He could look down from his "heavenly" place and view all that was happening in the physical world of ever increasing population.

How could Satan build a palace in the spirit realm? He used materials found in the earth's atmosphere.

Some of his captains and their troops were making their abode underneath the ground in large caverns. Others made their homes in the underground seas where they distressed the subterranean creatures God had placed there.

Most of Satan's demonic kingdom, however, spread across the surface of the earth and in the air above to establish territories within the twelve major divisions governed by the twelve generals.

Gawg ruled the entire northern area that is now called Russia. Tulinedbar extended his wicked influence to the southern tip of Africa.

Balashtar ruled the large area east of the Euphrates River, including the land of Nod where Cain and his family lived. This demon's name means "terrible eruption." The worship of false gods erupted like a volcano in Cain's family and spread like molten lava in succeeding generations until it affected the whole human race.

Satan, Baalmeg, Elgitlar and Pubilentre still occupied and ruled the small area around Eridu and the Garden of

Eden. The garden was still there, although it was now overgrown with brambles, weeds and thick underbrush.

The Tree of Life and Tree of Knowledge of Good and Evil remained there also, as did the guarding angels and the flaming sword. Now and then, groups of people would go there, but were turned away by the angels.

Adam, now a hundred and fifty years old, would gather as many of his descendants as would visit him and tell them about the garden, his sin and God's instructions for worship.

Seth was now twenty years old. His mother, Eve, gave him that name, which means "substitute," because she regarded him as a specific gift from God to replace Abel, whom Cain had murdered.

Adam and Eve gave a lavish wedding for Seth and presented Pelenadad to be his wife. Her name means "Wonderful, beautiful love." Indeed, God's love would be manifest through her because one of her descendants would be Jesus, the Savior.

Meanwhile, Satan was watching all these events with great interest and plotting how he could foil whatever plans God might have for these people.

Satan spent quite a bit of time sitting on the throne he had constructed for himself. It was black and heavy and fitted with wheels so it could be moved about. That way, Satan could go here and there to observe things and conduct meetings without leaving his throne.

The arms of the throne were decorated with serpents, whose fangs seemed to threaten all who approached. Serpents were also engraved on the wheels, the sides and the back. At the top of the high back, a fierce likeness of the Prince of Darkness himself glared down at all those who bowed before Satan.

A portable desk on wheels could be rolled up to the throne where Satan would write mandates and rules to govern his dark kingdom. A file cabinet was built into the desk to temporarily hold documents he had just written or had requested from the permanent files.

Satan was busy writing a memo to Balashtar one day when Pubilentre came, bowed low and said, "Master, Commander Radahniyr is outside with one of his minor subjects who wants to talk to you."

"Send them away," growled Satan. "I don't have time to listen to any minor demons."

"But Sir," pleaded Pubilentre, "he has been trying to see you for a month. He finally convinced a lieutenant to speak to his commander. His commander took him to their captain and then to the general. The general immediately sent them to me. His story is so important I think you ought to hear it yourself."

"Oh, very well, send them in," replied Satan.

They were ushered in and instructed to bow all the way down before Satan. They did so and remained there until he ordered them to rise.

Glaring at the cowering demon, Satan demanded, "What's your name?"

"Girnob," was the timid reply.

Satan looked at Commander Radahniyr and smirked, "Girnob? His name is Girnob? This frightened freak is named Girnob? Do you know what his name means?"

"Yes, Master," replied the commander. "It means 'cause to burn.' When you hear his story, you will see that it is a very appropriate name."

Turning his piercing gaze to Girnob, Satan asked, "And what is so important that you just had to see me personally?"

Girnob composed himself a bit and slowly spoke. "Master, I have found the place where the spirits of humans go when they die."

"What?" exclaimed Satan. "We have wondered about that for a great many years. How did you discover that?"

"Well, Sir," answered Girnob, "I was watching when a man named Lamech killed a teenage boy. I saw the boy's spirit leave his body and I followed it to the opening of a cave."

"A cave?" interrupted Satan. "It went to a cave?"

"Yes, Sir," replied Girnob. "One of the subterranean demons met him there and dragged him inside. I followed to see where he was taking him."

Satan pushed the portable desk aside and leaned forward to the edge of his throne. His eyes widened. His hands gripped the serpent heads on the arms of the throne. Saliva dripped from the corners of his mouth. His full attention was riveted on the face of Girnob.

"Yes? Yes?" he slobbered. "Then what happened?"

Girnob continued, "I followed them down, down, down, below the water table, below the seabed, down to a depth of about twelve miles beneath the surface. It seemed to be near the earth's upper mantle."

Satan excitedly inquired, "What did you find there?"

"Well," Girnob answered, "I'll try to describe what I saw. We came to a great wall with two large gates. From one gate emanated a heavenly perfume and beautiful music. Behind the other gate I could hear a sound like roaring flames and anguished screams.

"The demon knocked on the second gate. It opened and I followed as he dragged the boy inside. There was a path going downward. The boy began struggling violently and begging to be released. The demon lifted him up and they both floated down toward what was the most frightening scene one could ever imagine."

"What was it? What was it?" demanded Satan.

"It was a horrendous furnace of fire," said Girnob. "It stretched as far as I could see. Several humans who have died in the last hundred and fifty years were in the fire and could not get out. Their screams were so pitiful I had to put my hands over my ears."

"Then what happened?" inquired Satan.

Girnob shuddered, hesitated for a moment and then replied, "The demon threw the boy into the fire and shouted, 'There is no escape. You will burn forever and ever.' I think that is what may happen to us someday."

"Shut up, you fool! Shut up!" shouted Satan. "I don't want to hear that kind of talk. We are not going to be cast into any fire. We are going to win this thing. Do you hear me? We are going to win."

"Yes, Master," said Girnob. "I apologize to you. Please forgive my miserable mouth."

"I forgive you," replied Satan. "Now, I want you to lead me to this place. Pubilentre, get Baalmeg and Elgitlar. We are going to take a look for ourselves."

When the other two elqandeas arrived, Satan roared, "Why wasn't I informed of this place long ago? Don't my subjects tell me anything anymore?"

Pubilentre explained, "Master, we didn't know about it either. Those subterranean troops must have assumed we knew and just went ahead and did what had to be done. They should not be censured. They should be commended."

"Well," retorted Satan, "we'll certainly ask them about that when we get down there."

Away they all went, flying across the Euphrates and the

Tigris rivers, Girnob leading them to the cave and down into the bowels of the earth.

When they arrived at the wall, they knocked on the gate Girnob had entered before. It opened and they went inside. They looked around to see if they could find anybody in charge. Hearing the gate close, they turned to see a demon there. "What is your name?" inquired Satan.

"I am Showar, the gatekeeper," he replied.

Satan demanded, "And who put you in charge here?"

Showar explained, "An angel from heaven informed several of us that we could take turns standing guard to see that no humans escape."

"Why wasn't I told about this?" Satan shouted.

Showar answered, "We told our superiors. We thought you knew."

"Good work," said Satan. "I see you have my interests at heart. I will make sure you are rewarded. I shall also appoint a captain to oversee this whole area. Let me think, now. What shall I call it? Hmmm. Ah, yes, I shall call it 'hell.' Oh, the fun we can have with that word."

They walked around for a while until they came to a great chasm over which they could not pass. "What is this?" Satan inquired of the gatekeeper.

"Oh, that is to separate the bad people from the good people," he replied. "The humans here cannot go over there and those over there cannot come here."

Satan inquired, "Why are some of the humans over there? They are all under the condemnation of sin. Shouldn't they be over here in the fire?"

"I don't know all the reasons why," answered Showar. "I just know those humans are called 'good people' and these in the fire are called 'bad people.' That's all the information I have."

Satan turned to his three officials and said, "I don't like the looks of this. Every human that has died is supposed to be damned. There are no 'good people' as far as I am concerned.

"I'm going to find out what kind of trick God is trying to pull here. Come on, let's go to the other gate and take a look over there."

Back up the path they all went. Out that gate and over to the other they marched. They pounded loudly on the gate and waited. Slowly it opened and there stood a mighty angel, holding a glowing sword. "What do you want?" he asked.

Satan replied, "We are here to examine this place and see who is here."

"You are not permitted to enter here," said the angel. "You must leave at once."

Satan's eyes blazed and his mouth curled. He snarled, "How dare you speak to me like that? I am an archangel. Stand aside."

"Stop right there!" commanded the angel. "Come one step farther and I will make you wish you had never been created. Now, back off."

Satan shouted, "I shall report you to the Almighty Himself. What is your name?"

"My name is Elrogan," he answered. "I watch over this garden."

Pausing for just a moment, Satan calculated what he would say next, then asked a question. "Do you not know that I hold the title deed to the earth? I have every right to be here. You are trespassing on my property. Stand aside and let us pass."

The angel stood firm and replied, "Michael told me that I am not to argue with you or rail against you or accuse

196

you. However, he said the Almighty Himself authorized me to bind you and cast you into the fire for seven years if you try to force your way in here.

"Lucifer," he continued, "I suggest you take your friends and leave. I further suggest you limit yourself to those activities specifically allowed you by your Creator. You will not enter this part of Sheol."

Satan pointed his finger in the face of the angel and sneered, "You have not heard the end of this." He turned and growled to his companions, "Come on, let's get out of here."

Chapter Twenty-Two

How You Have Fallen

Satan and his demons made their way up to the surface of the earth, grumbling and complaining, cursing and blaspheming. Satan announced, "I am going to go up to God and demand some answers. I don't like this 'good people, bad people' stuff. They are all bad. They have all sinned. They should all be damned to hell."

When they reached the mouth of the cave, Satan dismissed Commander Radahniyr and Girnob, while he and the other three traveled on to Eridu.

As they approached, Pubilentre exclaimed, "Look, there's an angel in front of the palace."

Elgitlar added, "It looks like Michael."

"Yes," agreed Baalmeg, "I'm sure it is."

Satan increased his speed, flying over the Euphrates River and descending abruptly to face the mighty angel waiting there.

Michael said, "I've been waiting for you to return."

"What are you doing here?" shouted Satan. "This is my place. You have no right to be here. Get out!"

Michael replied, "The earth and all that is in it belongs to God. He created it. It is His. He created you and you have no rights or authority except what He gives you."

Satan commanded the three officials to bring his throne out for him. They rolled it out and he sat upon it, raising it upward into the air so he could look down on Michael.

He positioned himself arrogantly and glared at the angel standing there before him. "I am king of the earth," he snarled, foaming at the mouth.

Michael stood there for a moment, looking at him. Lucifer didn't look at all like he did when he ruled the Third Estate in heaven. His face was dark, his features hard. He seemed a bit smaller than before. His hands had a claw-like appearance and his feet were beginning to take on the shape of hooves.

The light and life of God were missing from his being. The foul smell of death and decay were already evident. What looked like horns were just beginning to grow from his head.

All of this change had taken place in Lucifer in less than two centuries. Sin was changing him from the image of God into something vastly different, something ugly, rotten and disgusting.

At last, Michael spoke. "Lucifer, Lucifer, how you have fallen. God created you perfect, but you have destroyed yourself."

"Shut up! Shut up!" shouted Satan. "Get out of here, Go back to your sniveling and groveling at His feet. You are not welcome here."

Michael continued, "I have come to answer your question about hell and paradise."

"You? You came to answer my question?" Satan lowered his voice and stared directly into Michael's eyes. "When I want answers, I shall get them directly from Him, not from one of His cowardly slaves.

"Pubilentre," snorted Satan, "escort this 'servant of the Most High God' to the upper atmosphere and send him on his way."

Michael said, "Lucifer, please listen."

"Get out of my sight," screamed Satan. "Get out! Get out! Get out!"

Michael turned and ascended, Pubilentre following close behind. When they reached the upper atmosphere, Pubilentre asked, "Will you tell me the answer to his question?"

"No," replied Michael. Pubilentre watched as Michael increased his speed and disappeared into space.

On his way back to Satan's dark palace, Pubilentre wondered, "Is there any possible way I could leave this place and go back to heaven? Would they accept me? Would He forgive me? No, I guess my only hope is to help Satan win this war for the souls of humans."

About a week later, Satan left his three top officers in charge and made the long journey to the gates of heaven. Speaking to the Chief Gatekeeper, he asked to see God.

"Do you have an appointment?" the gatekeeper asked.

Satan replied, "I don't need an appointment. Open the gate and let me in."

"I'm sorry," explained the gatekeeper, "but you cannot come in without official permission."

"You go tell Him I want to see Him," barked Satan.

The gatekeeper said, "Very well, I shall inquire for you."

Satan paced back and forth outside the gate while waiting for an answer.

After some time, a written reply was received. The gatekeeper said, "Here is a message from the Throne-room. It reads, 'Michael was sent to you with the answer to your question. Your pride has defeated you again. Now, you must wait until you can conduct yourself properly or until you are summoned by the Almighty.' It is signed, Pladmordan, Chief Attending Angel."

The gatekeeper turned and went about his business, leaving Satan standing there, protesting loudly.

Meanwhile, back on earth, Adam was speaking to Seth and his wife. "Most of my children are moving away to build their own cities. They are quickly falling into sin and abandoning my instructions for worshiping God. I hear that some of them are worshiping animals and trees, the sun, the moon and the stars.

"Please, my son, please stay close to me. Raise your children to worship God as I have taught you. God told your mother in the garden that one of her children would crush the head of the serpent.

"I have a feeling that you are that child. If not, maybe one of your children will do it. I don't know exactly what God meant, but I think it might have something to do with forgiving our sins and restoring us to the fellowship we had with God in the Garden of Eden."

Seth promised to do the best he could. Time would reveal that his descendants were rebellious against God also. However, a few of them would remain somewhat faithful to God.

When Satan returned to his throne at Eridu, he called a meeting of the twelve generals and the one hundred and forty-four captains. Pubilentre, Baalmeg and Elgitlar arranged them in a semi-circle before Satan's throne.

Each general reported the status of his division and the success his troops were having in occupying their territories. Although most of the generals did not yet have any humans in their territories, they were preparing to deceive them as they migrated farther and farther away from the godly influence of Adam.

Satan spoke to the assembled group. "Our problem is getting more serious than we anticipated. I need your absolute commitment. Each of you generals must make sure that every human in your territory is damned.

"Our efforts to kill all the humans are not going well. We must increase our war against them. I am going to call each general in from time to time and give specific instructions for each territory.

"Right now, we have another pressing problem. Angels are coming to earth in increasing numbers. They are hindering our attacks on the humans. I want each general to assign a captain with all his troops to form a shield around this planet. Do not allow any more angels to come here."

Satan ranted and raved for about an hour, then dismissed the officers. He called Pubilentre, Baalmeg and Elgitlar into his throne-room to discuss a number of ways the humans might be tempted to sin. He scheduled future meetings to plan more ways to kill the humans through disease, accidents and war.

Elgitlar went to get reports from the demons that were watching Adam and all those residing in or near Eridu. He returned to inform Satan of something he heard.

"Master," he said, "I heard from one of our troops about a conversation Adam had with his son, Seth. Adam told Seth that he thought either he or one of his children might be the one to crush the head of the serpent.

"We all know the snake you used in the garden died many years ago. We also are certain that God was speaking directly to you on that fateful day. Could it be that Seth or one of his children may do something that will break your power and authority?

"Is it possible that those in sheol who are called 'good people' are just waiting for this child of Adam to overthrow your kingdom and deliver them from the penalty of their sins? Could their sacrificing of lambs to God have something to do with all this? Surely, the blood of animals cannot atone for sin."

Satan paused for a long moment. His thoughts raced. His mind frantically sought some answers.

Then, he spoke. "Elgitlar, I want you to personally see to it that both Seth and his wife die before they have any children. As of now, that is your top priority. Pubilentre and Baalmeg will assume your other duties until you have killed those two."

Elgitlar made a temporary residence for himself on top of Seth's house. He enlisted a captain and two commanders to help with his assignment. The invisible realm around the house became a beehive of demonic activity that the humans could not see or hear.

Seth busied himself planting a garden beside the new home he had built for his bride. Adam gave him some sheep and cattle and cautioned him to offer only the finest of the flock as sacrifices to God.

Pelenedad decorated the house and devoted herself to pleasing her husband. She longed for the day she would conceive and bear a child for Seth.

One day, Seth came in from his labors and told his wife, "Honey, I have had an uneasy feeling for several days. I feel like we are being watched. I feel like something awful is about to happen. Do you feel uneasy?"

"Yes," she replied, "but I thought it was just me. I didn't know you felt it too."

Seth looked around inside and outside the house. He then said, "I think we ought to talk to Adam about this. Come on, let's go see him now."

Elgitlar slipped down from the roof and followed the worried pair as they walked toward Adam's house.

Publisher's Note: We hope you have enjoyed reading this book. The next book, "Man, Oh, Man, You Have Fallen Too," begins where this one ends.

The population rapidly increases. The human race plunges into corruption and sin as Satan's attacks intensify. Is there no hope for humanity? Will Satan win his war against God? Or, will God do something to rescue at least some of His creation?

"Man, Oh, Man, You Have Fallen Too" will show some of early man's discoveries and accomplishments as well as his slide into bondage to Satan. The birth of Noah causes great consternation in the Kingdom of Darkness.

We sincerely hope the second book will provide you with reading as exciting and informative as this first one.